WITHDRAWN

BIONIC

BIONIC

SUZANNE WEYN

SCHOLASTIC PRESS
NEW YORK

Fitchburg Public Library
5530 Lacy Road
Fitchburg, WI 53711

WITHDRAWN

Copyright © 2016 by Suzanne Weyn

All rights reserved. Published by Scholastic Press, an imprint of
Scholastic Inc., *Publishers since 1920.* SCHOLASTIC, SCHOLASTIC
PRESS, and associated logos are trademarks and/or registered
trademarks of Scholastic Inc.

The publisher does not have any control over and does not
assume any responsibility for author or third-party websites or
their content.

No part of this publication may be reproduced, stored in a
retrieval system, or transmitted in any form or by any means,
electronic, mechanical, photocopying, recording, or otherwise,
without written permission of the publisher. For information
regarding permission, write to Scholastic Inc., Attention:
Permissions Department, 557 Broadway, New York, NY 10012.

This book is a work of fiction. Names, characters, places, and
incidents are either the product of the author's imagination or
are used fictitiously, and any resemblance to actual persons,
living or dead, business establishments, events, or locales is
entirely coincidental.

For my darling Bill Gonzalez, who first suggested this idea to me and then texted pertinent articles daily. Thanks!

Oh, brave new world,

That has such people in it!

—William Shakespeare, *The Tempest*

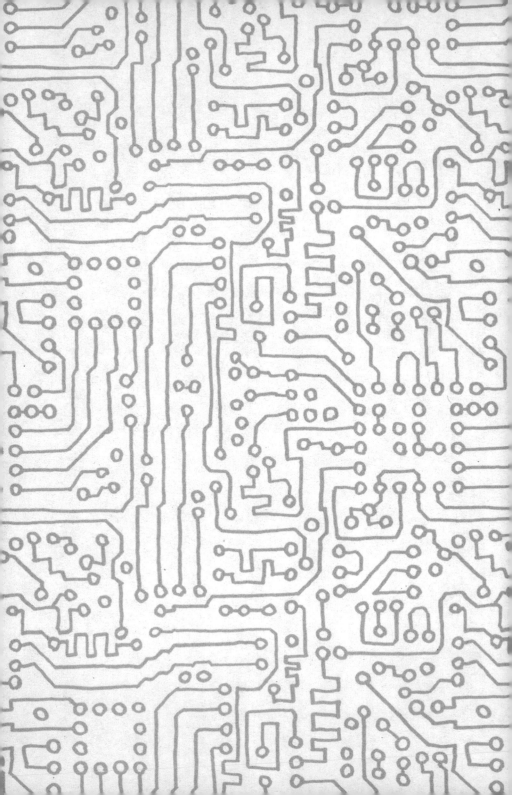

1

APRIL

I shift on the balls of my feet and lean toward the action on the field. The inside of my face guard mists with sweat as I watch Leanna hurtling over the midfield line, cradling the ball in the net of her stick. The other team's defense is close on her. We had such a solid lead in the first half of the game, but it's dwindled to a tie and gone into overtime. I can feel the tension of the game curling my shoulders, and I push them down, breathing deep.

"Mira!" Leanna shouts, and whips the ball over. Catching it, I see a clear shot, so I slam the ball past the goalie.

Yes! Tie broken! Finally! Moon Valley High wins it!

My team erupts into joyous shouts. Before I even know what's happening, they hoist me onto their shoulders and carry me around the field. My cheeks ache from smiling as I pump my lacrosse stick victoriously.

This feeling—it's the same thing I experience on stage, singing and playing guitar with my band, Electric Storm. That adrenaline rush, the wild enthusiasm of the audience, the sense of being a part of a bigger being that can make music out of nothing. It's magic! But maybe if I can have lacrosse, I won't miss performing. No. Who am I kidding? I'll miss being part of Electric Storm like crazy.

At the end of our last game, Coach Sanders pulled me into her office. I'd scored the winning goal then, too, and was relieved. Usually I'm one of the best players on the varsity team—but I'd been so off my game, and worried that I wasn't pulling my weight. Coach said I was wrong, that I did have a shot at a lacrosse scholarship, if I'd only buckle down with practicing and schoolwork. She said the band was distracting me from the things I'd need to get ahead. She insisted I quit Electric Storm.

From across the field, I catch Coach Sanders's warning expression. Going berserk over a win isn't considered good sportsmanship. Immediately, I jump down. My teammates follow my lead as we hurry over to line up for the handshake with the other team.

The moment I'm off the line, Coach Sanders takes hold of my upper arm and leans in. "See the scout from Penn State over there?" she says, pointing with her chin. "She asked about you. I told her I expect great things. You're on her list of girls to watch."

"Ohmigosh, that's awesome!"

"You bet," Coach Sanders agrees.

Some of the girls on the team wear ribbons on their upper arms to show that they're already committed to certain colleges. I haven't been approached with an offer yet. But my performance has been so much better this year than last year. This interest from Penn State is huge. It's finally happening!

"They're division one in the Big Ten," Couch Sanders says. "Keep playing like this and I think you'll have an offer by next month. Were you planning on applying to Penn State?"

Syracuse University and Penn State are my boyfriend Jason's and my top two choices. They have everything we want: division one teams, great academics, and a perfect location, far enough from home, but not so far that we have to fly. "I've already applied," I tell her.

Coach Sanders smiles at me, maybe for the first time ever. "Thatta girl! How are your grades?"

"Above average," I say truthfully. "A's and B's."

"Get 'em higher," she says. "Make this last quarter all A's. Beginning of senior year, too. You quit that band, right?"

I nod, though my heart sinks a little. When we formed the band, my friends Niles, Tom, and Matt dreamt about becoming rock stars. But we also just loved to play—enough to devote hours to practicing and talking people into letting us perform at parties, weddings, you name it. "Tonight's my last gig."

Coach Sanders holds me in a narrowed, skeptical stare.

"Honest!" I say.

"I hope so!" she says with a warning edge to her voice. "From now on you are about lacrosse and schoolwork and nothing else."

My hand shoots up as though I'm being sworn in at court. "Only lacrosse and schoolwork from now on," I say. I mean it, too! To blow off this chance would just be stupid. There and then I promise myself to fully commit to getting into Penn State.

The late bus pulls into the parking lot, snapping me back to reality. If I don't make the bus I run the risk of missing my younger brother Zack's bus, and I need to watch him until Mom gets home.

I jog across the field toward my bag, which contains my change of clothes. I'll have to take my stick with me. There's not even time to stow it in my gym locker.

"Aren't you changing, Superstar?" Taylor asks. "We're going to the diner."

"Can't," I say without slowing down. "I have to be somewhere."

Taylor falls into step with me. "You're not going to band practice, are you? I thought you quit."

"Who told you that?"

"Jason."

Wait . . . why is Taylor talking to Jason?

"Oh, when did you see him?" I ask.

"Like, yesterday?"

Jason is allowed to talk to whomever he wants. It just seems odd to me. I didn't think they were that friendly. At least not on Jason's side.

"No, I quit the band," I say.

"That must be hard for you," Taylor says brightly. She's put on that fake smile I've seen her wear so often. "Now you can only be a superstar in one area instead of two."

I slide my eyes at her. Was that meant as some sort of dig? I never can tell if she doesn't like me or just says dumb things, because she says it all with a smile.

"I'm just kidding, of course," Taylor says, still smiling.

• • •

"No! No! I can't eat that." Zack clamps his fingers into fists and pounds the sides of his legs. He glares at the tuna salad sandwich on the kitchen table as though he's Superman and I've just served him a plate of Kryptonite.

Okay. I run through all the variables in my head. I've seen my bother eat tuna a thousand times before, so it's not that. And I made it with the squishy white bread that he loves. "I didn't put carrots or celery in the tuna," I tell him. "It's plain with extra mayo, the way you like it."

"It's wrong," he insists.

I try to always be patient with Zack, but my voice rises in frustration. "What's wrong about it?"

Zack goes into his all-too-familiar *I'm not listening* mode, turning his head away from me. When he draws in his lips and narrows his eyes like he's doing now, he looks more like an old man than an eleven-year-old boy.

"Just eat the tomato soup, then," I coax him.

He shakes his head and continues to stare through the doorway into the living room. By now I kind of understand how he thinks. The soup goes with the sandwich as part of a whole meal, and the sandwich is somehow unacceptable, rendering the entire meal no good. Autism has a logic all its own.

Suddenly I see where I've gone wrong.

Lifting the plate from the table, I return to the counter and make a new sandwich. This time, though, I cut it on a diagonal, the way they do it at the Moon Valley Diner. It's the way Mom always does it here at home, too.

When I set the recut sandwich on the table—success! Without a word, Zack settles down to eat. I sit beside him, relieved, and consume the rejected sandwich.

What goes on in his head? He knows everything about insects and yet struggles through school, even with the help of an aide and outside tutors. Most of the time he's in his own world and then, out of nowhere, he's unexpectedly affectionate—for a brief while, anyway. Like he is right now, as he gives me a quick, wordless hug before making a beeline for the couch and a thick book titled *Lycaenids: From Chrysalis to Maturity.*

I dash upstairs to shower off the sweat and grime of the game. I wish there was time for a nice long soak in a bath, but I want to get ready for Electric Storm's last gig and don't want to leave Zack by himself so long.

My ripped, faded jeans are the ones I always wear when I perform, and once I pull on my T-shirt and scuffed boots, I'm dressed and ready to go. When I get downstairs, Zack is doing his homework at the coffee table. It takes all my self-control not to text Mom and tell her to hurry up.

Instead I text my best friend, Emma, to remind her about the show tonight. She wanted to come, but it's farther away than most of our other gigs and she said she might not be able to find a ride, which I totally understand.

The second Mom walks through the door, I'm on my feet, grabbing my bag.

"Did you two have something to eat?" she asks.

"Of course," I tell her, as she pulls me into a hug. "See you tonight!"

She tells me to break a leg, and as I run out the door I see her settle on the couch with Zack. "So, what's new with the lycaenids?"

. . .

When I get to Matt's house, his mom's van is idling in the driveway. The guys are leaning against it. "Sorry! Sorry!" I say before anyone speaks.

But there's not a lot of conversation as we load up the last few pieces of equipment, just some grunting. It's hard to tell whether it's better or worse than when I had to tell them I was quitting.

"We don't want anyone else!" Niles cried.

"Who else would do that weird little dance move?" Matt put in.

"What dance move?"

"You know," Niles said as he started stretching and writhing. Was that an impression of me?

I punched him on the shoulder. "I never do that!"

"Sure you do—during the drum break in 'Urban Creep.' It's cool."

My face warmed and I hoped I wasn't blushing. "That break is so long. I have to do something."

"Where are we going to find someone else like you?" Matt asked.

This, of course, was *exactly* what I wanted to hear—that they couldn't go on without me, that no one else could ever replace me.

Matt threw himself over his drums, pretending to sob in loud rolls of fake crying, and Tom joined him. Niles, though, looked like he might *really* cry, even though he didn't.

Just thinking about it makes me start to choke up. This is really happening. Tonight's my last time playing with these guys.

My phone buzzes as Matt closes the trunk of the van, and it's a text from Jason. **I'll be there tonight with some of the guys. Good luck on your last show.**

I decide to shake off the funk I'm in. The band is great, but not if it stops me from going to college and getting out of this town someday.

Thanks, I text back. **Big news. Penn State here we come!** I'm finally focused on my future and know what I have to do. I'm eager for this last Electric Storm gig to be over so I can pour myself into my schoolwork and lacrosse.

The guys climb into the van ahead of me and I sit up front next to Matt. This is our usual arrangement, since I'm the best at using the map app on my phone.

Matt barely listens to the directions because he knows how to get to Yonkers. But when we have to find Midland Avenue, he gets nervous. I can tell from how tightly he grips the wheel while a thin vein in his forehead pulses. Now we're in unknown territory.

"In six hundred feet, turn right," my phone instructs in its robotic female voice.

"How am I supposed to know how far six hundred feet is?" Matt snaps.

"It's coming up soon," I say as the program counts down the footage. "Turn here!"

Matt curses as he sails past the street.

"Hang a U-turn at this gas station," I suggest.

Matt swears again, peering over his shoulder to where he should have taken us. "Okay," he mutters, barely slowing down as he whips the van into the Shell station.

But he's too fast. And he doesn't realize that a gas tanker is backing up.

"Matt! Stop!"

Crunching metal explodes around me. Shielding my head, I cower into the seat.

Matt's forehead slams into the steering wheel. From the backseat, Niles clasps my arm for a second but his hand is thrown off as the van spins.

It bashes into the truck again. It's tilting! The van is tipping.

We're going over!

Matt's limp hand slaps my cheek when we hit the cement. My face is pressed on the window and the cracked glass slivers my skin.

A car slams into us, spraying more glass. Searing, unbearable pain consumes me. I let out an agonized scream that merges with Niles and Tom's tortured swearing from the backseat.

A jagged piece of bloody steel from the door pierces my thigh and now it sticks out the other side.

The rancid odor of hot rubber. Black smoke.

A shrillness wails.

. . .

Sirens. Swirling red light. A sudden surge of cool air as a mask goes over my nose and mouth. That's good. A gentle voice asking questions. I turn my head toward it. Agony. Too much pain. Can't stay like this! Leaving . . .

. . .

I sit in a kayak in the middle of Lake Oscawana, near our house. The sky is indigo streaked with vivid pink. Ribbons of golden light cross it. No one else is on the lake. I'm not rowing, just sitting there with the paddle laid flat in front of me. A pleasant warm breeze ruffles my hair.

The first time I paddled my own kayak, I was five.

My mother's voice booms across the surface of the water. "When Mrs. Frederick C. Little's second son arrived, everybody noticed that he was not much bigger than a mouse." The words are the opening of the book I loved most when I was small, *Stuart Little*. She reads on and on for a long time as I sit in the kayak, listening.

A lovely day.

"I love you, Mira."

I'm so tired. Everything around me starts to fade. All I want is to sleep . . . sleep . . . sleep . . . and sleep. To disappear.

Leaving.

Where have I been? It's confusing. I was gone and now I'm back on the lake. I lie on the raft attached to buoyed ropes in the little-kiddie beach. Small kids splash and laugh on the shore. They're too far away for me to see clearly.

Gazing up into the brilliant blue sky I hear a voice coming from a cumulus cloud. Sitting up, I wonder who's speaking.

"They say maybe you can hear me, Mira, so, here goes. I'm in the room upstairs from this one. I'll probably go home today or tomorrow. I'd have come to see you sooner but they only let me out of bed today."

Niles.

"I had a punctured lung and I'm in a cast up to my hip, but I'll be all right. Matt fractured his nose and has some horrible burns. The second car went on fire. We were lucky it wasn't the fuel truck. Really lucky. We wouldn't be here at all right now if that had exploded. Tom broke some ribs, and has some cuts. They say the person in the passenger seat always gets hurt the worst, and you did. We're all so . . ."

The voice, Niles, trails off, which is a relief. I'm glad everyone's going to be fine. I feel fine. Super relaxed, actually. But I don't want to hear about broken bones and burns right now. I'd rather stare at the lake.

Zack reads to me from his book on butterflies. Normally that would bore me, but out here on the lake everything is interesting: lightweight sailboats gliding by; gentle breezes rippling the surface of the water; dragonflies darting everywhere.

Zack's voice pours out of the clouds like honeyed sunshine. I'd like to see him but he's hiding behind the clouds.

I never realized how soothing Zack's voice is. I picture the butterflies emerging from their cocoons, like newborns, wet with new life, spreading their gorgeous wings.

• • •

I tread water as three fish swim circles around me, jumping above the surface of the sparkling lake. They take turns reading *Frankenstein* and all sound like Jason.

"You'll need to have this read for the AP lit comprehensive test at the end of the year," says a silvery-green fish, bobbing his head.

A blue-green fish jumps before he speaks. "You won't be here forever. You should be prepared."

"Come on! Wake up, Mira!" the third, slightly boggle-eyed fish shouts.

• • •

My hair fans out around me. Lake water splashes into my face. I've discovered that if I pull both my arms behind my head, my toes rise. If I lower them, they sink. It's sort of a fun game, watching them rise and fall. I recall learning that this has to do with finding my personal center of gravity.

I like the sound if it. If I find my center of gravity I will be able to float endlessly.

After a while, though, the water no longer hits my face. I stop floating and tread the ever-diminishing water as the lake gets lower and lower. Soon I am stranded on cracked, arid earth.

The bright blue sky blisters like old wallpaper. I can see behind it.

Florescent light explodes everywhere. The drone of machinery fills my ears.

My mother is there. She sleeps, curled in a chair. A stone-faced nurse enters the room and becomes wide-eyed before she hurries out.

My body is on fire. My head is being slammed against a cement wall. My mouth won't release the scream trapped inside it.

Take me back to the lake.

I want to go back to the lake. I'll find my center of gravity.

And I'll float endlessly.

• • •

Under water, watching the lake go by above me.

• • •

Woke up back in the hospital room but no one knows I'm here. I hear them bustling around, though. I want to alert someone that I'm back, but I can't speak. My eyes won't open, either.

Emma sits beside me. I know she's there but she doesn't know I know. "Don't cry," I want to say as she lays her forehead on my arm and sobs. But I can't because . . . I just can't.

· · ·

Mom is beside my bed and she softly sings a song that I haven't heard her sing since I was small. "Hey! Mr. Tambourine Man, play a song for me . . ." She sings more and hesitates. I know the line she's trying to recall.

"Jingle jangle," I whisper.

Silence.

What's happening? My eyes slide open and Mom is bent over me, staring.

"Doctor!" Mom shouts. "I need a doctor!" She grips my hand. "Stay with me, Mira! Stay awake!"

The pain is too awful. I can't.

Let me go back to the lake!

"Stay awake," Mom begs.

"Doctor!" Mom shouts, pounding buttons over my bed.

· · ·

MAY

The hospital room is where I live now. Morning and night I'm here, drifting in and out of sleep. I can't remember the way back to the lake.

. . .

My room is soft with gray light. It's either very early or getting dark. I see myself reflected in the TV near the ceiling at the end of my bed.

I'm wrapped in bandages . . . but something's very wrong with the shape of me. Where is my arm?! It feels like it's there but it's not.

I just can't see it. That's all! The glare bouncing off the TV set is covering it. My cell phone is on the nightstand to the right of my bed. I want to text Jason and Emma to tell them I'm awake, so I stretch forward to pick it up.

Why can't I reach it? It's too far away. I stretch farther.

My hand isn't even near the phone. I should be seeing my hand next to the phone, fingers stretching. It doesn't make sense! I don't understand.

And then I *do* understand.

My right arm is gone.

My right arm is gone!

I can feel it but it's not there.

With my left hand I pound the call button above my bed.

A nurse hurries in with another woman, a doctor wearing a white coat and stethoscope. I don't realize how truly, mind-meltingly freaked out I am until I start jabbering hysterically, all the while gesturing wildly with my left arm.

"You've had a terrible accident," the doctor says kindly as she takes the needle the nurse hands her. "And this is all very shocking. It's a lot to absorb. I'm going to give you a shot to help you calm down, help you to rest."

I can't rest! I want my arm. I'm enraged and the fury injects a jolt of crazy energy that lets me sit up and grab the doctor by her wrist. "Get me my arm!" I shout. It comes out as an animal growl. I must seem insane. Maybe I am.

Another nurse grips me while the doctor injects something into my vein. Writhing, I struggle to escape my body.

I want out! OUT!

But I relax almost immediately.

Calm.

I drowse.

Of course, I still need to ask where my arm has gone, but my tongue has grown fat and lazy.

I hope I'm going back to the lake, but I don't see it anywhere anymore, not even in my dreams.

2

I have no idea what my last name is. I know my first name, because everyone keeps calling me Mira. Otherwise I'm not sure I'd even know *that*. Sometimes I remember Mom right away and other times I think she's my aunt Jane. Or maybe Aunt Jane did come to see me. I'm not sure. Confusion has become a way of life.

"You're very lucky you were wearing your seat belt," says one of the anonymous doctors who pass in and out of my room all day and night.

That's debatable, I think. Maybe if I hadn't been wearing my seat belt I'd be dead right now. The idea of being dead has definite appeal. I know that's a morbid thought, but depressed and angry and terrified thoughts are all I have these days. Otherwise I sleep and dream about a gigantic oil truck running over me again and again until I'm sawdust in the road.

• • •

No one visits me besides Mom and Zack. Now that I'm out of a coma, no one is allowed. There's no cell service in here, either.

That's all right. I don't feel much like talking. Most of the time my head hurts.

Zack reads me more books about butterflies than I ever thought existed. In my imagination, they race around the room in a swirl of color. I become one of them. When I'm lost in the world of butterflies I can forget everything.

Mom finishes *Stuart Little* and goes on to *Charlotte's Web*. She must think these books are comforting or that I'm in no shape to deal with anything more adult. Mom's right on both counts. I love *Charlotte's Web* except that nearly every night I dream I'm a fly struggling mightily to escape a web. Each morning I wake up exhausted and sad.

JUNE

This morning, like every morning, I wake up uncertain of where or who I am. I'm a newborn blinking at the fluorescent light, completely baffled by what's going on.

Slowly, though, it all returns to me . . .

The anesthesia . . . *count backward from ten . . . three . . . two* . . . So many operations. The constant pounding in my head, the continual nausea. The constant beeping of machinery, the buzz of people talking somewhere off in the distance. The television noise that never seems to end. At night a blinding light might suddenly snap on. An aide wants a blood sample, a nurse needs to change my intravenous bag. The electrodes on my chest and stomach must be changed. All this is how I live now.

Here's what's happening, as best as I can remember. (Warning: My best is not that hot these days.) My right arm has been amputated from the shoulder down. I have no left leg remaining under the knee. The kneecap on my right leg needs to be replaced. These parts of my body were apparently completely crushed. My nose is broken and my left cheek is shattered. I have skin grafts where I was burned.

My entire head is wrapped in bandages. I see through an opening in the bandages. I breathe through another opening with the help of one of those breathing things you always see on TV.

As the nurse changes the intravenous bag of fluids I've been hooked up to all this time, she says, "There's a little extra something in here to help you sleep. We want you to be good and rested in the next few days."

Why? What's happening in the next few days?

That's the question I thought I'd asked, though maybe I only dreamed I'd asked it. In minutes, I'm in that black hole of nothingness I've become so accustomed to. It's a place where there are no dreams, no bizarre subconscious images, and no groggy struggle to wakefulness. It's a place where I've been erased. But I'm not really gone. Eventually I emerge once more into the world of harsh light and constant pain.

It's while I'm lying there, still not opening my eyes, that I hear Mom talking to a doctor. "Her state is desperate enough that she qualifies for the procedures," the doctor says. "As part of this test group, the operations and all the follow-up won't cost you anything."

"She's been through so much already," Mom says.

"That's the point. With all she's gone through, why not go the rest of the way?" the doctor asks. "As she is now, her life will be extremely limited. The damage to her limbs is only part of it. The brain damage alone will severely impact her functioning."

"In what way?" Mom sounds as alarmed as I feel.

"Continued deteriorating memory loss, emotional instability, loss of control over bodily functions. There's even a chance that, with the blow she took to the occipital lobe of her brain, her eyesight might begin to diminish."

"She'll go blind?!"

"It's possible."

"Can you really stabilize all that?" Mom asks hopefully. "Any of it?"

"Science has come a long way."

"But what are the dangers?"

"I'm afraid there are no certainties here. We've developed these programs in conjunction with the military to aid our soldiers, but we need trial subjects who haven't been in combat as a first line of experimental controls. She'll be receiving the cutting edge of what science has to offer."

"If she does all this will she ever live a normal life?"

"If she doesn't do it, her *normal* days are behind her."

• • •

I am rolled down the hall today, still in my hospital bed. We get to another room where a way-too-sprightly nurse gets me out of the bed and into a sitting position. "How are you feeling, Mira?" she asks.

A million snarky replies fly into my head, but it's too much effort to speak. It's just as well, since she's only trying to be pleasant. So I just nod, catching my reflection in the window behind the nurse.

"You're getting fresh bandages today," she tells me, as though she's revealed I'm getting a new convertible. "But first we're doing a few tests."

She unwraps the bandages from my head. It's been weeks since I've seen my face. And now I wish I hadn't looked. Half of my face is purple and green, a tie-dyed–looking swirl of hideousness. My nose is a mushed, pulpy mass and seems to have migrated somewhat to the left side of my face. My right cheekbone has caved in. What hair I have left lies snarled in clumps, plastered against my scalp.

Tears jump to my eyes. This can't be me. I don't even look human anymore. I'm a monster!

The doctor who was telling Mom that my normal days might be behind me comes in. He's heavy and bald, with a calm, friendly voice. "I'm Dr. Hector, Mira. You're here because we're putting electrodes on your head today," he explains in a this-is-no-big-deal way.

"So we're going to have to get rid of patches of hair. Would you prefer we just take it all off?"

I shrug. What do I care? My hair is the least of my problems right now. And how much more horrendous can it look than it already does?

He slides his hand along his polished baldness and smiles a little too broadly. "I find it very low maintenance. On girls it's kind of an edgy look."

Smiling dimly, I nod again.

"We want to look at your brain activity," He gets down to business as the nurse shaves my scalp. "A lot is going to depend on what we find out today."

"Like what?" I mumble.

"We need to find out if you've suffered brain damage, and if so, where and how much. We need to discover what you're going to be capable of going forward."

The nurse finishes her shaving and applies electrodes to my head. When she's done, I grab another glimpse of myself.

Between the electrodes and my broken cheek, I'm something out of a SyFy channel original movie. Frankenstein's monster wouldn't have needed a bride if he'd met me. He'd have been head over heels in love.

For the next hours, I respond to beeps and flash cards and small electric zaps while different sections of my brain light up— or fail to. It's intensely strange to watch my own brain do its thing on a screen in front of me. Until this day, my brain wasn't something separate. It was . . . me. At the very least, it was control central of me.

But seeing this brain imaging changes everything.

Am I my brain? Or is my brain only a part of me?

If I am my brain, am I no more than a unit that reacts when different parts are poked and zapped? What if I don't want certain brain sections to light up when they show me a photo of Mom or Grandma Lynn or Aunt Jane or Zack? Do I have any choice in the matter?

It's been a long day of testing and I'm too exhausted to ponder these questions much more. In my room I admire my new crispy white bandages. *I look so much better!* I mean to be snide, but it's actually true. The bandages are an improvement. At least they hide the repulsive thing I've become on the outside.

• • •

I'm forgetting what my friends look like. What do *I* look like? I forget that, too.

I haven't looked into a mirror in a long time because I haven't been out of bed and my face is still covered in bandages, anyway. Since the most recent operation, they're new, fresh bandages. Every few days another operation. Lots and lots of surgery.

Sometimes I think I'm the Mira Rains of before the accident. In my dreams, I'm that girl.

But who will I see when I'm finally able to look into the mirror?

• • •

"You're going to like this better than your previous leg and old foot," says the young, cute doctor named Dr. Tim. We're in a room of the hospital and I'm in a wheelchair. He pulls up his khaki pant leg to reveal a rod that goes down into his sneakers. "I have a match on the other leg, too."

I saw him walk in the door and I never would have guessed.

"I used to be a championship rock climber," he says. "Then one night I was stuck up on the ridge of a mountain after dark and frostbite got both my legs at the knee."

I furrow my brow and frown. "That must have been scary as anything," I say.

"I still climb. It took a lot of PT, of course."

"What's that?"

"Physical therapy," he explains. "And you know what? I wouldn't trade my old legs for these. These are better."

I shoot him a narrow-eyed glance of disbelief.

"I kid you not," he insists.

Dr. Tim opens a guitar-case-sized container sitting on the floor. In it is a metal leg very similar to the ones he wears. I stare at it in horror.

"We're going to fit you for one of these today," he says.

I can't imagine something this cold and metallic strapped to my body.

"Don't look so horrified," Dr. Tim says, smiling. "You're going to get to love this thing. It's state of the art. Beyond state of the art! But this isn't your final leg. It's just to get you started."

"How long until I get the final one?"

"We'll wait until you're completely healed, so we get an accurate final fit."

"When will that be?"

"You're young and you'll heal more quickly than an adult. I'm guessing six months."

Six months! That seems ages away. I'll be a senior in school. I can't imagine what my life will be like in six months.

Dr. Tim tugs up my sweatpants to where the stump of my knee is covered with gauze bandages, which he carefully unwraps. The sight of the scarred, twisted flesh makes me turn away. "It's okay," he says kindly. "I've seen worse. They did a good job. The swelling has gone down almost completely, so we can get you set up with the temporary prosthesis for now. That's the one I showed you."

Dr. Tim takes measurements. He places a stretchy soft cover over the stump. It looks a lot less upsetting with the cover. "My assistant will take some more photos, we'll get some digital measurements, and we'll start a mold," he tells me.

A woman around Mom's age dressed in green medical scrubs smiles at me as she enters. "You're going to have to learn new balance and coordination," she tells me. "It'll take a lot of work, but it will be worth it. We'll give you exercises. It's important that you do them at home, as well as during PT."

"Will I ever be able to play sports again?" I dare to ask.

Dr. Tim bounces on his artificial legs. "I'm going rock climbing this weekend."

"Can you run?" I ask.

"Try to catch me."

. . .

The staff doctor, Dr. Thomas, is in her thirties with long straight black hair. She snips my head bandages gingerly with a scissor. They stick to my skin a bit as she lifts them away. There's some pain when I flex my facial muscles, they've been immobilized for so long.

I yawn and then attempt to smile, as she instructs. It's somehow painful and good at the same time.

"Ready for a mirror?" Dr. Thomas asks.

That's a good question. Am I ready for this?

Dr. Thomas smiles as she lifts a hand mirror from a nearby table. "It's really not that bad, Mira," she says. "It will improve every day, so don't panic."

Panic!? There's a reason to panic? I reach out to take the mirror from her. I have to know.

My face is still so black and blue, especially under my eyes! Not to mention I'm still bald. (Well, not quite. A smattering of stubbly hair covers my scalp.) My nose is less mashed and they've somehow maneuvered it back into the center of my face. That's something, anyway.

A nurse comes in to place new gauze over my concave cheekbone. "They're going to fix that tomorrow," she says as she works. "You'll have nice high cheekbones like a model."

"That will look weird—one high cheekbone."

"They'll make sure your cheekbones match."

When the bandaging is finished, the nurse slides me into a wheelchair. Mom comes into the room and walks me around the hospital. It's good to be out of my room and to see people who smile sympathetically as I pass. A very old man stoops to pat my hand. "It will be all right, young lady," he says. "You'll see."

He has no idea if it will be all right or not. But I want to believe he knows what he's talking about. His kindness touches me and a lump forms in my throat.

• • •

Today, as I struggle to come awake, I hear something rustle under my hospital bed and I scrunch into a ball. It has to be mice.

But it's too loud to be a mouse. A squirrel? A rat?

Sucking in a deep breath, I stretch over the side of the bed to see.

And come face-to-face with Niles Bean!

He slides out from underneath. His eyes laugh as he holds his index finger to his lips. "I snuck in," he whispers, drawing the privacy curtain around my bed. "I had to crawl past the guy at the front desk."

He digs in the khaki-colored canvas bag he's got slung over his shoulder. "I made you a present," he says. He extracts what at first seems to be a doll. "Ta-da!" he sings out, presenting it to me.

I can't believe what I'm looking at. It makes no sense.

"It's you!" he says.

It *is* me. I'm performing with the band, doing the dance they were teasing me about at rehearsal, my arms stretched, bent at the waist, my head thrown back.

"How?"

Niles chuckles, delighted. He sits closer to me on the bed. "Three-dimensional printing," he says quietly. "Pauling has 3-D printers now." Linus Pauling High School is the high-priced, very progressive school Niles attends. They always have the latest and the greatest everything. "Mira, you won't believe it. They're, like, the coolest things you've ever seen."

"But how do you make something like this?"

He pulls a crumpled photo from his bag. It's of the band performing, the one with me dancing. "I scanned this into the printer and did some calculations about the dimensions. They're teaching us how to do it. The printer can figure out what the 3-D form will look like. Our particular machines are printing with resin, but some use plastic. There are others that even use sugar. They can print with almost anything."

I turn the image in my left hand, marveling at it. "Thanks, Niles! It's awesome."

Niles grins happily. "Isn't it cool?!"

"Beyond cool."

A nurse peeks through the curtain, and unfortunately she's one of the crankier ones. "I thought I heard talking," she says when she sees Niles. "Out you go, young man."

"Do I have to?" Niles wheedles.

"Yes, you do. Don't make me call security."

"Don't worry. I won't. Could you hand me my cane?" I see the piece of wood that's resting on the floor.

The nurse scoops it up, handing it to Niles. The top of the cane has been carved into a man's head. The handle is formed by the red stocking cap he wears above his grouchy, scowling face. "It was my grandfather's," Niles explains with a smile. "Cool, huh?"

"Very," I reply truthfully. "Will you always need it now?"

"Nah," he dismisses my question with a wave, "just until I'm out of this cast."

"How long will that be?"

Shrugging, he pulls himself to standing, leaning on the cane. "Who knows?"

"Young man," the nurse prompts him to get going.

"Bye, Mira. Feel better," he says.

The space between us grows thick with emotion. I think he's about to bend in to kiss me. He doesn't, though.

I wave as he hobbles out. For the first time in what feels like a lifetime, I smile.

My phone buzzes and it's Jason. I'm awash in guilt for having wanted Niles to kiss me just now. What kind of awful girlfriend am I?

JULY

"Think of this as training wheels on a bike," Dr. Tim says. We're in his examining room in the hospital. I'm in my wheelchair wearing my fake leg under my sweat suit. He's peppy and upbeat, as always.

"Training wheels for my wheelchair?" I ask lightly. What's he talking about? "I don't need them. This thing doesn't tip."

He smiles at me. "No, training wheels for you!" He takes a cloth off a stand to reveal a series of rods and wires attached to a robotic hand. It's attached to a cast of my upper body that was made five days earlier by a combination of digitized measurements and plain old-fashioned plaster mold-making. "It's a pretty basic prosthetic." He picks up what looks like a TV remote. "You can control it remotely with this, and we're also going to get you a harness that will help your strong shoulder control the movements."

Dr. Tim aims the remote at the arm and the delicate jointed fingers open. He pushes some different buttons and the fingers curl into a fist.

"Cool," I say.

"This is nothing," he tells me. "Right now we want you to get used to using it. We need to make sure the fit is perfect, that it's not too heavy for you. It's a start."

"What comes after this arm?" I ask.

"We're working on way cooler stuff than this. You'll see."

Dr. Tim leaves as Carol, his assistant, comes in to help me put on the arm. I catch sight of myself in the full-length mirror hanging over the door. I look like a robot with all the rods and wires. Why did this happen to me?

A tear slides down my cheek.

Carol rubs my shoulders. "I know, honey," she says in a sympathetic tone. "It's a lot to handle."

For some reason, the kindness in her voice sets me off. Fat tears flood down my face. It's so embarrassing and yet such a relief to cry. I can't stop it, anyway.

"Let it come, Mira," Carol says, handing me a box of tissues. "Just cry it out, sweetheart."

A lot of tissues land in the wastebasket before I'm done.

There's a knock and Dr. Tim waits for Carol to say it's all right to come in. He stops short when he sees my face. "What's this about?" he asks.

"Just an emotional moment," Carol tells him gently.

"Aw, come on," Dr. Tim says. "This is exciting! No reason for tears. When we're finished fixing you up, everyone will be jealous of you."

"I doubt that," I say with a thick, shaky laugh.

"You wait," Dr. Tim says confidently. "You just wait."

. . .

"Keep coming toward me, Mira. Don't depend on the railings so much. Try to find your center of gravity." Raelene is the physical therapist assigned to my case. She's a muscular woman with a soothing voice.

I struggle at the center of two parallel bars, limping along, a titanium lower leg and fake foot on one side and an artificial knee on the other. I grip one bar with my real hand and leave my fake hand open and brush it along the railing. "Without the railings, I'll fall," I reply, sounding whinier than I intended. This is our fourth session and I've become an expert at falling.

"Keep your hands on the rails, but try to hold yourself upright with your abdominal muscles."

"What abdominal muscles?" My once-hard stomach has turned to mush after so many weeks of being in bed.

Raelene laughs. "Don't worry, you'll get them back. We're going to work you real hard, but in the end it will be worth it."

I nod, hoping she's right. "You sound like my lacrosse coach, Coach Sanders."

"It's good you're an athlete. You know about training for a goal. That's what we're doing here."

Shutting my eyes, I envision the lacrosse field. I have to get across, so I constrict my abdominals and squeeze my glutes as best I can. *Just go*, I command myself. My fingertips only skim the rails as I step out. Right foot . . . left . . . right . . . left.

My artificial knee crumbles and down I go at Raelene's feet. "Way to go!" she cheers, squatting beside me. "That's it. You got it!"

"But I fell," I say, disappointed.

"It's all baby steps," she says. "You're learning to balance all over again, like a toddler does."

I have a new respect for toddlers. This is work! Frustrating, exhausting work. It's demoralizing and humiliating not to be able to do the most basic of activities. I can't stand, walk, or even control my new arm. By the end of the day, I'm once more in tears.

3

I thought the day would never come, but today Carol pushes me to the front door in my wheelchair. Mom is right behind me, loaded down with medications and paperwork and bags.

When Carol stops inside the front door, I lean heavily on my crutch and pull myself to standing. The weeks of exercises I've done with Raelene have built up my back and abdominal muscles to the point where I can hold steady and not tumble forward.

Suddenly I feel unsteady and I clutch at Mom's arm to keep from going over.

"Don't worry," says Carol. "We'll be seeing you in just a few days for some more PT and tests."

I grab a look at myself in the hospital's glass door. Mom bought me some cute overalls that I wear over a flowered peasant shirt. The cheekbone that's been replaced with a surgical implant is noticeably larger than the other, though they tell me that the swelling will go down. My nose bends where it was broken. The bruising is almost gone, but faded patches of bluish purple still run under my eyes and across the bridge of my nose. The skin grafts on my arm and chest still look raw.

When the electronic door slides open I breathe in fresh air for the first time in over three months. There's a warm breeze tossing the trees. It smells like maybe rain is coming. Until this moment it never really hit me how much I've missed living in the outside world. The hospital has been my home for so long that this morning I was strangely nervous about leaving. But all those anxieties vanish in a moment, as this real world comes rushing in at me.

Mom leaves me on a bench while she gets the car. My phone buzzes and I use my left hand to fish it from the pocket of my overalls. Jason has sent a text: **I'll come over as soon as I'm done caddying. Is that OK? I can't wait to see you.**

Hurry over! I write. But I suddenly panic. What will he think when he does see me? It never crossed my mind when Niles sneaked into my room. Does it mean that I really do think of Niles as a friend, while to me Jason is still my boyfriend? It might. It's confusing but strangely comforting. At least it clears things up. Jason is my boyfriend and Niles is a friend on whom, admittedly, I had a little crush.

At the moment I'm very concerned about what my boyfriend will think when he sees the new Bride-of-Frankenstein me.

• • •

Emma waits outside my house, waving, when Mom and I pull into the driveway. Arms flung wide, she runs to embrace me but does a quick dance of awkwardness when she reaches me.

"She won't break, but be gentle," Mom says.

Emma kisses my left shoulder. "I'm so happy you're home." She helps Mom carry my suitcases into the house, then returns for me. "Are you in pain, Mira?"

"I'm used to it," I say. This is part not wanting to complain but mostly true. Everything hurts, all the time. Right now my cheekbone is the most painful part. It's radiating a throbbing ache that runs across my face and travels up to the top of my skull. The other worst pain is that my leg prosthesis is causing my hip to ache.

Inside, Emma hands me a gift wrapped in purple tissue paper. It's a pastel drawing of the lake. "I made it for you because I know it's your happy place," she explains. "I wanted to give it to you so you could look at it while you were in the hospital, but I didn't finish on time."

"It doesn't matter," I tell her. "It's beautiful. You're so talented!"

Emma beams and impulsively wraps me in a hug that throws me off balance. She catches me as I stagger backward and then hugs me again. "I'm so glad you're home, Mira!"

"Me, too."

"I went back to see Madame Suza again," Emma tells me, dropping her voice so my mother, who's in the kitchen, won't hear.

"Why would you do that?" I ask. Our first visit with

the psychic, Madame Suza, hadn't exactly been a dazzling success—she'd made some huge, dramatic deal of not telling me what she saw in my palm, probably to scare us into paying more, and we'd left pretty annoyed. I was surprised Emma would spend any more money on a fake psychic.

"After everything that happened to you, I couldn't stand it anymore. I had to know what she saw in your palm that day."

"What did she say?"

"She saw the accident."

"In my palm? How?"

She turns over my palm and traces her finger along a crease. "This is your lifeline—and see, it has this sharp line across it. Then look how it starts wandering all over your hand. She says that's not normal. It means your life will be disrupted in a major way and never be the same again."

"Why couldn't she just tell me that?" I ask.

"She—that wasn't the upsetting part." Emma seems uncertain whether or not to continue. "She saw a big number fifty-six over your head and says it means change."

"That's not a big deal," I say. "Obviously things have changed."

"She had a vision that you changed into a creature with a giant head."

"Ew," I say. We stare at each other for a minute. This is too weird. "Well, Madame Suza is a kook. I wouldn't take it too seriously."

"No! Of course not. No!" Emma says. "I shouldn't even have told you."

"That's all right."

"It's just stupid."

"Totally stupid," I agree. I embrace Emma using my left arm. "I've missed you," I say.

"Me, too."

"I brought you something else," she says, handing me a large wrapped package.

"Thanks, Emma!" I say excitedly pulling off the paper with my left hand. It's a gorgeously illustrated copy of *The Tempest* by Shakespeare. Different artists have illustrated different chapters. I'd been admiring it back in April when we'd been in the mall bookstore together. The story about a wizard shipwrecked on a desert island with his daughter is pretty cool, but I'm especially interested in *The Tempest* because my name, Miranda, was created by Shakespeare just for the play.

We sit side by side on the couch, paging through it. Emma sighs. "I wonder if I'll ever be as good as these artists."

"You're already awesome," I say sincerely. "Imagine how great you'll be if you go to college to major in art. I mean, I've thought about what you said, and I don't agree that college isn't for artists. Think of all the art classes you'd be taking. You'd love it."

"You might be right," Emma agrees thoughtfully. "There would be a chance to study different techniques. I don't think I'd ever get as good as these guys on my own. I wonder if they went to college."

"We could Google it."

"I wonder if they have classes in songwriting in college. You could definitely study poetry."

"You could illustrate your own poems," I say.

"No! I'm thinking about you and your songs for the band."

Will I ever perform with the band again? My days with the band seem like another lifetime. Who was the girl who could jump around, dancing wildly? It doesn't seem possible it could have been me.

I yawn, suddenly exhausted, and Emma rises from the couch.

"You're probably tired," she says. "When's the last time you made it this far from a hospital bed?"

Before leaving, she kisses my fake cheek, and I yelp in pain. "Sorry! Sorry!" she says, her voice an anxiety-filled squeal. "I'll be more careful."

• • •

After an hour-long nap, I sit on the living room couch waiting for Jason. I've put concealer over the bruising from my broken nose. It's only partially successful.

When the doorbell rings, Zack answers it.

"Hey, big guy!" Jason's voice carries from the entryway.

"Hey," Zack replies listlessly.

When Jason turns into the living room and sees me, he stops, shocked.

He's speechless.

I stand up abruptly, thinking my crutch will hold me, but it falls to the side and I drop to the floor. Not exactly the most graceful move.

Jason flies to my side, flustered and panicked. "Mira! Are you all right? Should I call someone? An ambulance?"

"I'm all right," I say, sprawled on the floor. "I just feel like an idiot."

"No! No! Don't feel that way. Are any of your . . . uh . . . fake parts . . . broken?"

Suddenly I'm concerned. I hadn't considered that possibility. "Help me up and I'll check," I say. He helps me get reseated and—as he watches, wide-eyed with amazement—I stretch out my fake arm and raise my prosthetic leg, swiveling my jointed ankle. "It all seems to work," I tell him.

Jason is mesmerized by my prosthetics. "Can you wiggle your toes?" he asks eagerly.

Pulling the sneaker off my good foot, I wiggle my good toes. Jason stares at my foot, then up at me, and then back at my foot. "That's incredible," he murmurs, awestruck.

"That's my real foot!" I shout. "I'm just messing with you!"

Jason is instantly red-faced. "Don't do stuff like that, Mira! How am I supposed to know?!"

"I'm sorry!" I can see that he's nervous and doesn't know how to act. "Really, that was mean. Sorry."

"That's okay," Jason says, gathering his composure. He bends to examine the fake leg. "That's amazing! How do you like it?"

I shrug. "Okay," I say. It's better than having no leg. The window air-conditioning kicks on with a *thunk*, which is welcome, since I'm starting to sweat. We sit on the couch, both unable to think of anything to say.

After a while Jason reaches for my left hand, but it's a stretch and it's awkward, so he lets go.

"How's your summer been?" I ask.

"Okay. Fine. Caddying."

I nod.

"I would have come to see you if they'd let me," he says. "You know that, right?"

I nod again.

"And your phone never worked, so . . ."

"I know, it's fine."

He notices *The Tempest* on the coffee table. "This is next month's assignment for AP lit this year," he says. "You can get a start on it."

I'm not taking AP literature anymore, I don't think. I'll be lucky if they even pass me on to senior year after all the school I've missed. "I've read it," I remind him.

"You have?" He raises a surprised eyebrow.

"I watched a movie version with Mom and it has my name in it, so I got interested to read it."

"Your name?"

"Yeah. Miranda, remember?" There's a sharp snarkiness in my voice that I didn't intend.

"I just think of you as Mira."

"That's short for Miranda," I say. "I've told you that."

"I just forgot."

"That's okay," I say, though my cold tone says otherwise. Why am I picking on him? Maybe I'm still tired.

Jason picks up the book and thumbs through it. "Emma brought me the book. She was here just before," I tell him.

"I should have brought you something," Jason says. "I'm sorry. I didn't think of it."

"That's all right," I say, trying to be more pleasant. "The important thing is that you're here. I'm glad to see you. Sorry if I was crabby with that thing about my name. It was stupid."

"I know your name, it was just that—"

"Forget it! It was me."

Jason leans in to kiss me, as he normally would. I lean forward, too. Jason hesitates, then kisses my cheek. Thankfully it's my good cheek—the left one. "I'll text you later," he says.

Jason blows me a kiss before escaping out the front door. Unexpected tears rim my eyes as he leaves. What did I expect? That everything would snap back to normal once I got home? I mean, how unrealistic is that? But, I suddenly realize, it's exactly what I expected.

4

Leanna texts, offering to visit. She arrives with a carton of Ben & Jerry's (Phish Food, my favorite!). We eat the ice cream at the backyard picnic bench while she fills me in on who is dating whom, and who's breaking up, and what everyone has been doing over the summer.

"Taylor broke up with that boy she was dating for, like, a week," Leanna says. "She has no luck with guys."

"Why do you think that is?" I ask.

Leanna shrugs. "No idea. She's cute. It's not like she doesn't try. She's always after some guy."

"Anyone in particular she's chasing now?" I ask, thinking of how she flirts with Jason.

"Not that I know of. So, how are things going with Jason?" she asks as she licks the back of her spoon.

"Fine, I guess." Why did she mention Jason?

"You guess? He's been to see you, right?"

"Yeah."

"Is it weird with all the . . . changes?"

"You mean the fake arm, broken nose, lumpy cheek, and red,

twisted scar on my nearly bald head changes?" I want to take a lighthearted tone as I say this, but I realize it's coming out a little intense. "I'm sorry," I apologize. "I didn't mean to sound so weird."

"It's totally understandable. You've been through a lot," Leanna says. She gives an ironic laugh. "That's kind of an understatement, isn't it? I mean, I can't even begin to imagine what you've been through. It's not like I know, but I imagine it's been horrible for you."

Leanna checks her phone and starts to rise. "I have to get going. There's a lacrosse meeting about who's going to be team captain next year. I want to let Coach Sanders know I'm interested." She hesitates. "You won't be playing, will you?"

"I don't know. Maybe. I hadn't really thought about it."

She shoots me a skeptical look, which I understand. I sure don't *look* like I'll be playing a sport anytime in the near future.

"Well, see ya soon," she says with a little wave. "Feel better."

I wave back as she disappears around the corner of my house. And before I really think about it, I'm dialing Jason's number.

"Hey, babe," he says when he picks up. "Everything okay?"

"Is it?" I ask. "Between us, I mean?"

"Whoa, where did that come from?" he asks. "Of course we're okay. You've been through hell and back, but we're still solid." There's a little pause. "Want me to come over?"

"Would you? That would be great."

I should feel better, knowing my boyfriend loves me so much that he offers to come over when I ask him to. So why do things still feel so unsettled?

• • •

Jason's visit makes me feel better. He brings a gift in a small box. "I wasn't planning on seeing you today, so I didn't get a chance to wrap it," he says. "But you sounded like you could use some cheering up so . . . open it."

It's a pretty bracelet with M-I-R-A-N-D-A spelled out in beads.

"I wanted to prove I really know what your name is."

"You just want me to wear it in case you forget again," I tease him.

He pretends to be offended. "I never forgot it."

"I know you didn't," I say. "Thank you. It's very pretty." I hold out both my fake hand and my real one. "I wonder which wrist I should wear it on."

He knows I'm messing with him again and rolls his eyes. "That's up to you."

I slip it on the fake wrist. "There, that's . . ." I was going to say *cute* or something like that, but I'm unexpectedly ambushed by my emotions. The bracelet with my name on it on my robotic wrist suddenly strikes me as hideous and sad. I begin to cry.

Jason puts his arm around me. "I thought you liked it," he says.

"I do like it," I say through my tears.

"Then what's wrong?"

"I don't know," I admit. "Maybe I should have put it on the other wrist. I thought it would be funny but . . . it's not."

Jason slips it off my robotic right wrist and onto my left. "There," he says. "Is that better?"

Wiping the tears from my eyes, I nod. "I feel silly," I say. "I really like the bracelet. I'm so emotional these days. Everything's so difficult. I don't know if I'll ever get back to normal."

Tears well up again, but I don't want them to. Everything makes me cry these days. Everything.

• • •

After Jason leaves, Mom comes in holding shopping bags. "Wait until you see the things I got you," she says happily, unpacking the bags. "I found this cute yoga mat, some weights, these stretch bands." She pulls out a box containing a blow-up stretch-and-balance ball. "We'll have to find a pump to blow this up. I think there's a bike pump in the garage. That might work."

Looking up, she stares at my bland expression. "What?" she asks.

"Do you want me to use this stuff right now?" I ask.

"Raelene says we should start right away. She gave me the list of equipment to get. You're going to have to get really strong to use these prosthetics."

"I was strong before I got hit by a fuel tanker."

Neither of us speaks. The memory of it is too awful.

Mom shakes it off and returns to unpacking. "I was thinking that in addition to your regular PT and at-home exercises, you might want to try a yoga class. We could take it together on the evenings I don't work late. It could be fun." She pulls flowered stretch pants from the bag. "I found these cute stretch pants for you."

They're hideous.

"Do you like them?"

"They're cheerful. Thanks."

Mom tosses the pants to me. "Go put these on and we'll get started. I think abdominal crunches are the first thing. I could use some of those. I'll do them with you."

"Do I have to?" I'll admit. It came out as a whine.

"Raelene told me to start right away. This is crucial to your recovery, Mira."

"I just got home," I argue. "Can't I have a little time to adjust to things?"

"Raelene said—"

"I'm sick of Raelene!" I shout. "I'm sick of doctors, and nurses, and IV tubes, and bedpans, and being told what to do every two seconds." I know I'm being horrible, but I can't help it. I just explode.

"Mira, I know it's not fun but you have to—"

If one more person says, *you have to* do this or do that . . . I'm going to completely lose it. I've done everything everybody has been telling me to do for months now. I can't stand it another second. "I don't have to do *anything* I don't want to do!" I shout at Mom.

The expression of shock and distress that appears on Mom's face almost undoes me. But my outburst feels so freeing that I don't want to stop. Not sure what to say or do next, I grab my crutch and make my usual watery retreat to the bathroom.

If I don't get into some water right away I feel I'll explode.

Only now, to do this, I have to struggle to take off the artificial leg. I have to do it using my fake arm and hand, which isn't easy. Taking off the harness that helps hold my arm and then getting the arm off is even more difficult.

"Do you want help?" Mom calls from outside of the bathroom.

"No. I've got it." Do I? We'll find out. Sitting on the edge of the tub with the water running, I lower myself.

And then I lose my grip and slide down with a thump against the tub. The water is rushing in but I can't pull myself above it.

Mom's there immediately, pulling me out of the tub. Water splashes everywhere. Thank goodness I didn't lock the door. Throwing a large bath towel around my shoulders, she gets me settled on the closed toilet lid.

She starts crying, which unleashes my tears. I can't even get into the bathtub on my own!

"I shouldn't have let you try that by yourself. It's my fault. I'm sorry," she says through small sobs.

A horrible choked sound comes out of me. I can't even bathe myself!

When she wraps my robe around my shoulders, I struggle into it. "Thank you."

"This will all get better, Mira," Mom says. "It won't always be like this."

I nod, but tears stream down my cheeks.

5

AUGUST

Zack knocks on my bedroom door and I look up from *The Tempest*. I'm actually just going through the drawings, which are really gorgeous. There's one of Miranda, the wizard's daughter, sitting on a rock, gazing out at a stormy sea, that I really love.

He sits on my bed, showing me what he's holding. It's a picture frame about the size of a lunch tray. There's no picture under it, though. Instead, there are about twelve luminous, multicolored butterflies somehow attached to a board.

"It's for you. It just came," Zack tells me. "I spent all my birthday money, but it was worth it."

Looking more closely I see that the Latin name of each species is typed below. Each butterfly is different from the next. "Who found all these?" I ask.

"Butterfly catchers, I guess. Each of these began as a caterpillar," Zack says.

"I know," I say. Metamorphosis is a shocking change, if you think about it: ugly little creatures creeping along the ground, turning into glorious flying insect angels. And all that hard work of metamorphosis, only to be captured by some greedy butterfly collector. Gassed and glued to a board.

"Are you crying?" Zack asks me.

I didn't even realize I was. "No," I say, wiping my eyes.

"Do you have a cold?" he presses me.

"Yes, a little cold," I reply.

"I don't think it's a cold. I think the butterflies are making you sad," he says, and I'm shocked because he's usually not this perceptive about feelings. "I didn't mean to make you sad. I thought you liked the butterflies when I read about them to you."

I hug the collection of butterflies to my chest. "I love these butterflies!" I say. "I love that you got them for me."

"Really?"

"Absolutely! Yes! You spent all your birthday money on this, really?" He nods.

Putting the frame beside me, I hug Zack to my side. "You're the best brother ever!"

"You're the best sister," Zack replies, smiling shyly up at me.

I tickle him with my left hand, which sends him into gales of laughter for a second. Then he pulls back into himself. "When are you going to start using your other side?" he asks seriously.

His question is surprising, but he's right. I've been doing everything with my left arm and hand. "I don't know. I suppose I should start practicing with my right."

"You can't just let it hang there. That doesn't make sense."

"You're right. It doesn't."

"I'm going to get a nail so we can hang this up in your room," Zack tells me. Just as he leaves, a text from Niles buzzes my phone. He's sent me an old video from *Bye Bye Birdie*. It's Dick Van Dyke dancing around singing "Put on a Happy Face."

There's no choice but to smile.

Corny! ☺ I text back.

But great!

Lol, I text. And though I'm not literally laughing out loud, I *do* feel cheerier. I'm lucky to have Zack, Niles, and Emma working so hard to make me happy.

The band has to start rehearsing again, Niles texts. **It's time.**

☹ **Not ready,** I reply.

Sure you are.

Maybe another time? Ttyl.

It was nice of Niles to send the video, and I feel bad about the way I shut him down. I have to try to be a little more pleasant to be around or no one is going to want to be around me at all.

My bedroom window is open and I can hear the cicadas making their chittery summer sounds. Thunder bangs around even though there's no sign of rain. Gazing out the window, a line of sparking lightning cracks open the sky. Then, more dry thunder, louder this time.

Hearing all this sound makes me wonder what sounds I can still make. I attempt to sing "Mr. Tambourine Man," a song I know so well I could remember the words even while in a semi-coma. Forget it! Horrible sounds scratch their way out of my throat. My singing voice is shot!

The sky suddenly opens, letting loose pounding rain. It soaks the windowsill. Getting off the bed, I reach for the window sash—but with my right hand. Using my left hand, I press the switch near the elbow of my right arm.

Up goes the arm. A second switch makes it stretch to the top of the raised window.

It's so odd to touch something, yet not feel it.

I press down but it doesn't budge. I can't judge the amount of force I need. I press harder. The window drops with a bang.

Getting used to this thing is going to require a lot of work. I'm not sure I have enough energy left to work that hard. This is all just getting to be too much. I want to forget about all of it, but of course, I can't.

• • •

"Feeling fatigued?" the hospital nurse asks. I've never met her before. Her name is Trish.

"Yes."

"How often?"

"Very often." Almost always.

"Feelings of hopelessness?"

"Depends on the day."

"Do you have more bad days or more good days?" Trish asks.

"I don't know. When I first got home everything just started to feel weird. It was like everything was the same, but nothing felt the same. And I'm scared of the future. What's there for me to feel hope about? I don't know how I'm going to get through school, which starts next week. I don't want to have to go back and have everybody staring at me."

"Do you feel people are staring at you now?"

"I've hardly been out of the house up until now. But I'm scared to go out. I don't want to feel like some sort of . . . some sort of freak."

"You're not a freak. It's normal to be anxious."

"It's difficult, you know," I say. "It's a lot of work. It's not fair. Why did this have to happen to me?"

"Do you think you might be depressed?" she asks.

Am I? Who wouldn't be? This whole situation is horrible. In the spring I was worried about getting a scholarship, now I'm worried about dropping the hand soap because I'm not sure I can stay balanced if I bend to pick it up. "Sometimes I want to give up and just sleep all day," I tell Trish honestly.

She writes something and then stands. "I'll be back in a moment."

When she's gone I lean across her desk to read what she's written. *Depression expressing as laconic behavior, feelings of hopelessness. Abandonment.*

The nurse returns with a prescription. "Try these twice a day," she says, handing it to me.

"What is it?

"It's a mood elevator combined with an anti-anxiety medication. I've just called your mother and she okayed it."

I fold the script and put it in my pocket, but I'm not sure how I feel about taking medication like this. Will I still be me if my outlook is artificially elevated? I hardly even look like the same girl as the statuette that stands on my bedroom shelf— the six-inch, 3-D–printed, dancing wannabe rock 'n' roll star. But inside I *am* still the same girl. I feel her feelings. My sadness is mine to feel. That person who is myself—I don't want her to go away.

What if even *that* disappears?

A fat tear travels down my face. I don't even feel it at first because my artificial cheek has lessened sensation. When it hits my chin, I wipe it away.

"It'll be all right," Trish tells me, wearing a kind expression for the first time. "The pills will make you feel much better."

· · ·

Okay. So, I *do* feel better. My mood, anyway. It took a while, but there's no denying that the pills finally started to work. I enjoy feeling better, too. I even had Mom drive me to a salon to have my eyebrows waxed for the first time ever because I can't manage to tweeze them with my left hand. (I even considered asking for a half-price deal on a mani-pedi but worried that the people in the salon might not get my humor.)

It's not that I'm unaware of what a disaster my life has turned into. But with the happy pills it doesn't hurt as much to think about. I'm more focused on the *what now?* than on everything that's been lost.

Maybe my less bummed-out mood is just another part of me that's artificial, but I'm living in the land of *whatever works* and I can't think too much beyond that.

The next *what now?* doesn't take long to appear. "I just talked to Dr. Tim," Mom comes in to tell me one morning as I'm sitting on the edge of my bed and strapping on my titanium foot. "They want to fit you for a new prosthetic arm next week."

"Really?" My calmness at this news is due to the pills, I'm sure.

Mom sits beside me. "It sounds wonderful, Mira! All you'll have to do is *think* about an action and your arm will do it."

"That doesn't make sense to me," I say. "How does it work?"

59

She reads from the notes she wrote on the back of an envelope. "It's called osseointegration. They'll insert a metal implant into the stump of your arm. Then they'll attach the prosthetic arm using wires and nerve electrodes." She turns over the envelope to read notes she's made on the other side. "Targeted muscle reinnervation uses computer algorithms to learn the patterns of the user's action and can begin to anticipate them."

"Like the predictive setting on my phone," I guess.

"Could be," Mom agrees. "Dr. Tim says that these new arms are so much lighter than ever before, thanks to the use of graphite and microtechnology. He says you're going to love it."

I smile. "He always says that."

"He was very enthused and wants us to come in today, if we can. I'll get Karen to cover the first half of my shift at the diner. I'll have them hold Zack at the After-School Center till I get there. Hurry and get ready."

"How long is this going to take?" I ask, leaning on my crutch as I stand.

"He said you'll be there overnight."

"And then lots and lots of training classes," I add.

"It will be worth it."

"It sounds worth it," I say. Thanks, happy pills, for the positive attitude. I'm glad to have it right now.

6

I leave Dr. Tim's office curling and uncurling the mechanical fingers of my new arm. Unlike my foot, it's covered in fake skin. My new fingers come complete with molded fingernails. If a person saw me with a short-sleeved shirt, about two inches of the rod would be visible. Other than that, no one would be able to tell it was fake, at least not unless the person was right next to me studying my hand.

Mom arrives back from the ladies' room. "It looks great. Let's try to shake hands."

It's startling when my hand juts forward and spreads its fingers wide to shake. I don't think I told it to do that—but I must have.

When I close my hand around Mom's to shake, she goes pale. Quickly I release her. "That's some grip you've got!" she says breathlessly.

"I'm so sorry, Mom!" When we look, I've left a red thumb mark on the back of her hand. I'd better be careful with the fist bumps and high fives. I might break someone's wrist.

"Dr. Tim emailed the school giving permission for me to go back. Here's a copy of it," I say, handing the paper to her with my left hand.

But Mom refuses it. "Try it with the right."

I'm sick of *everything* being a production. But I switch the letter to the other hand. It falls on the floor between us. "This is going to take some getting used to," I say.

My afternoon of fake-arm training goes very well. It doesn't take long before I have the correct grip down. Apparently my brain does that calculation automatically and once I get used to it the computer in the arm starts remembering. The only downside is a humming, whirring sound when my arm moves. It's not too bad, though.

I get a text from Niles. **We're rehearsing tonight. Come by?**

I miss seeing the guys, and all of a sudden I really miss hearing music, even though I haven't played it on my phone or in the car since the accident. And having the fake arm makes me feel good, so I agree. Maybe I *am* slowly getting better.

• • •

The band is all set up when I get to Matt's house for their rehearsal, and it's strange to go in after all this time. Months ago, I was walking in to quit. A few days later, we were on our way to a gig. A few hours later, my life changed for good. It takes me a few minutes and a couple of deep breaths, but I finally head inside.

Matt's nose is now crooked where he broke it. He has a little scarring from the burns. Tom looks fine.

Niles's cast is gone, but he's limping even with his cane. "Why are you still using that?" I ask.

"I don't know. My leg is just fine but my hip is weak for some reason," he says. "They think it's just a matter of regaining muscle mass, so we'll see."

"Are you getting PT then?" I ask.

"Yep. Twice a week."

"Good," I say. "Hopefully that'll help."

"You didn't bring your guitar?" Niles says. I sense he wants to change the subject.

"Give me a break! I just got this right arm today," I say. The guys cluster around, admiring it.

"Is it super strong?" Tom asks.

"It kind of is," I say.

"Want to arm wrestle?" Tom asks, joking.

"You'd lose," I warn him.

Matt circles me, staring at my arm. "That is so freaky cool," he says. "How does it feel?"

"In what way?"

"I don't know. In every way. You're almost a robot."

"Don't be such a jerk," Niles tells him harshly. "She's not even a little like a robot."

"Maybe a little," I allow.

"Yeah, but robots are mechanical. They don't have *feelings*," Niles says. He looks pointedly at Matt. "*Feelings* that can be hurt."

"Sorry. I didn't mean any offense," Matt tells me.

"It's okay," I say, waving it away with my left hand. "I'll look less robotic when I get a better leg, one that's more like my arm."

I sigh and recall the conversation I had with Raelene earlier today during PT. Once we finished with the new arm and hand, we did some walking exercises. Once again, as I tried to let go of the parallel bars and walk on my own, I came crashing down on my right knee, the one with the plastic kneecap replacement.

I'll still need the crutch even though I'd love to be done with it. The falling happens all the time and it's discouraging. I just haven't seen much improvement, and I don't know what else to do.

"Raelene, my physical therapist, thinks I'd be doing better with the fake leg and foot if the muscles of my other leg were supporting me the way they should."

"What do you do about that?" Niles asks.

"I don't know."

"Personally," Tom says, "I would *love* to be a cyborg."

"You would?" I ask doubtfully.

"Oh, yeah!" Tom's face lights with enthusiasm. "It's the future, man! We're all heading in that direction—have been for years. It's just that nowadays it's really possible."

Matt folds his arms thoughtfully. "I was watching this thing on the History Channel where they suggested that maybe humans are creatures created by alien cyborgs and have been intended to become cyborgs all along. We'll live hundreds of years as cyborgs with replaceable parts."

"Think about it, Mira," Tom says. "You're like the first of the new breed of human beings."

"Shut up, you geeks," Niles says. "Let's play!"

They begin and it isn't long before I'm bopping in my seat and getting the strong urge to sing along.

When they're done, Niles sits beside me. "Want to join in the next set?"

"No guitar," I remind him,

"Not a problem about the guitar. You can still sing, can't you?"

"Yeah, I guess so," I reply. Except remembering that sad little croak that came out of these vocal cords a couple weeks ago—I'm pretty sure I can't.

He hands me a tambourine. "Give it a try."

"Who's been doing the vocals?" I ask.

"Me," Matt says glumly, "and it's not great." This is exactly what I want to hear. They haven't replaced me and no one has done it better. They've missed me! Yay!

"Let's do 'Urban Creep,'" he suggests.

The guys begin playing, and I nod along to the intro. "Urban creep, from down deep, I see you even in my sleep . . ."

The guys look at each other warily. I'm not meant to catch their sideways glances, but I do. This isn't good.

My voice shakes. The tambourine beats are off. But I continue. Then I stop. I can't remember the words. I've sung this song hundreds of times, but suddenly I'm blank. "Sorry, guys," I say as they stop playing. "This has been happening since the accident. Yesterday I couldn't remember my address."

"Your brains got scrambled, huh," Tom remarks.

Niles shoots him a look.

My stuff is in a corner and I start gathering it up to leave, keeping my head down so that no one else sees how red my face is, or the tears I'm trying to blink away.

"Where are you going?" Niles asks.

There's no denying that I'm embarrassed. Mortified, actually. "I have to get home," I lie.

"All right," says Matt, shooting a look at Niles. "But we'll see you next time, Mira."

"You just need some time to get back into things," Niles says. "Maybe it's just too soon."

"Maybe," I agree halfheartedly. But it might always be too soon. If this is the new normal, I'm not exactly liking it.

• • •

Sitting by the living room window, I notice the patterns in everyone's days. The same people come and go at the same times. Old Jim next door walks his dog, Rusty, every morning at eight, then again at five. A day-camp bus drops the same two small kids off at four every afternoon. The mail carrier drops the mail in our box at two every day. In just two days I've got their routines nailed. Even the birds and squirrels show up at more or less the same time. I've never before realized how much of life is lived from habit.

These days I refuse my happy pills. After that disastrous rehearsal, I don't want to be happy, or even feel better. What's the point if I'm never going to be able to live the way I used to? If I'm never going to do all the things other people my age are planning for?

The doctors have patched me up as best as they can, but it's not good enough. I look hideous, I won't ever play lacrosse again, I can barely walk, my singing voice is gone, and my brain is a soggy, leaky paper towel. I've stopped reading because I can no longer remember what happened in the story before I put it down last.

If I just sit in bed, I won't have to struggle to remember things I've always known, or why I came into a particular room.

I'm drowning in pitiful looks and whispers. It's everywhere I go—*the poor girl. What could have happened to her?* People try not to stare, but it's hard not to. I can't blame them. I'm pathetic.

I even see it in Mom's eyes. *Poor Mira!* But today, her pity has shifted to worry. (I've become very good at telling the difference.)

I hear her in the kitchen quietly talking to someone. "I know it's for the best, but I wonder if she needs a rest from all this. I'll think about it. All right. I'll speak with her. Thanks. I'll call you. Bye."

"Who was that?" I ask from the living room after she hangs up. She comes in looking somber.

"I was speaking to Dr. Hector," she says. "He thinks you're doing well enough that—"

"He thinks I'm doing *well*? He's got to be kidding."

Mom sits beside me. "He is of the opinion that your physical recovery is proceeding faster than they'd expected."

"They must not have expected much."

"He wants to perform some more operations."

My head drops into my left hand. "No! Mom, please."

Stroking my hair lightly, Mom leans in to speak softly. "Listen to me, Mira. I know this sounds stupid, given how you feel right now, but you're a very fortunate girl. It's simple good luck that they happened to be looking for a candidate for these tests after your accident. You're being a given an opportunity to receive the most cutting-edge medical help in the world. And I want the world for you. I think that if we don't take a chance on some of these procedures, we'll ultimately regret it. I can't have that. We have to try. Can you try?"

What choice do I have? It means so much to Mom. How can I let her down?

"If you do this you'll miss a lot of school," Mom reminds me, "but it should bring some really major improvements."

How badly do I want to return to school? I definitely want to graduate on time. Hopefully I'll be able to catch up. I wouldn't mind some *major improvements* in my condition.

I look at Mom and nod my head. "Okay, Mom, you're right. I want to try."

7

This is a new place. It looks like a small private hospital. I think it's in Connecticut somewhere. Dr. Hector is the only familiar face. He wipes his hand over his gleaming skull. "Still got the cool hairdo going, kiddo," he says, smiling at me. I'm completely bald. Almost the first thing they did when I arrived was shave my head again.

They're implanting some kind of copper chip in my brain. They call it a neurotrophic electrode.

When I was a kid, I had a game called Operation. It's all I can think of as they wheel me to the operating room: the clown patient with the glowing nose that lights up and buzzes every time the player accidentally hits the side of the cavity containing his organs while trying to remove them. I'm so drugged up that I can't stay awake. I dream I'm lying on an operating table wearing a red nose. Dr. Hector is there holding a chain saw.

Buzz! Buzz! Buzz!

I hope they know what they're doing.

• • •

Another day, another operation. Today, cable yarn replaces my damaged muscles. It will be many times stronger than regular human muscle and will support my prosthetics more easily. If I become a superhero, am I responsible for saving the world? I hope not. I can barely save myself.

. . .

New knee day . . . Dr. Tim says that in combination with my cable yarn muscle, it will support me perfectly.

And get this . . . it's created by a 3-D printer using real cartilage and plastic. I text Niles to tell him. **Awesome,** he texts back.

He sends a picture of himself posing in front of the 3-D printers at his school. **If you ever need a spare part let me know.**

You make me sound like a junky old car, I reply.

Definitely not junky, he replies.

Thanks a lot.

JK! Good luck.

. . .

The area around my knee is swollen to twice the size it should be. It's hard to believe it will ever be as great as Dr. Hector says. "Give it time," Raelene tells me, and we work on bending and flexing my leg. Easy for her to say.

. . .

My eyes blink open again after my fifth surgery. Sixth? It feels like I've been unconscious for a long time—my throat is dry, and all my muscles are stiff. The pain in my right shoulder is especially intense.

An arm! There's what looks like a real arm there. No rod shows. It is attached to my shoulder as naturally as my original flesh-and-blood arm.

Despite being groggy, I sit up. It doesn't appear as human as my last prosthesis did. It's clearly mechanical, with visible cable yarn muscles bound together in a metal casing, and part of me wishes I could go back to the old one, which at least needed a second glance before anyone could see it wasn't my real arm.

I think about holding on to the rails of my hospital bed. My fingers wrap effortlessly around the metal, without sliding off or clutching too tightly. But here's the amazing thing: I can *feel* the rails. They're cool. I touch my hospital blanket. It's soft. The skin on my right arm is smooth.

My robotic arm goes to my mouth as I gasp with emotion. My breath is warm on my palm.

"Be careful with that thing," Dr. Hector says, coming into my room. "It's a lethal weapon."

"What?"

"We have to calibrate it. Right now it's extremely strong, much stronger than the last one. Wiggle your fingers."

They're just like real fingers.

"We implanted an electronic copper chip in your brain and it's transmitting signals from your brain right to your nerves. It's an implanted computer."

"So now I've got a robot brain?" I say.

"Your brain is still your brain," Dr. Hector says, "but, Mira, kiddo, let's talk. That copper chip in your head is also helping your heart pump more strongly. We've implanted a few other internal devices to help you manage all this new stuff in your body. This will all take some getting used to."

"Like how?"

Dr. Hector draws a thoughtful breath as though deciding how to answer. "The truth is, we don't really know. We're counting on you to report to us how you're feeling, and we'll be taking baseline tests at regular intervals. We'll all be talking a lot, and making sure everything's working smoothly. These experiments are of major importance to a lot of people, returning veterans in particular, but also anyone who has ever lost a limb."

"What if I become a psycho killer now?" I ask, only half joking.

Dr. Hector smiles. "We're not anticipating that as a possible outcome."

"Good," I say warily. "Tell that to the police when they come for me."

"I wouldn't worry about it," Dr. Hector says. "But seriously, have you noticed any strange or worrisome symptoms after all these operations?"

I shake my head. "Am I getting a new, improved leg and foot, also?" I ask.

Dr. Tim comes into the room. "Soon," he says, "As soon as you've adapted to your new arm and hand." I remember that Dr. Tim rock climbs with his prosthetic feet. "Will I ever be able to play sports again?" I ask.

"You can get fake feet fitted for running and a different one with webbed toes for swimming," Dr. Tim says. "We even have one with built-in cleats—are those allowed in lacrosse?"

"I would guess so."

"Think about it," he says. "You don't have to decide right now."

"Okay."

"And we won't have the same hairdo anymore," Dr. Hector adds. "Now that we're done with electrodes and such, you can let your hair grow back."

"Yay," I say with a little clap.

Dr. Tim says good-bye. When he's gone, Dr. Hector looks at me seriously. "How's your mood been?" he asks. "I know they gave you something for depression."

"I stopped taking it."

"Why?"

I'm not sure exactly. I was feeling better with it. "I think part of me wanted to be depressed. But then, gradually, I began feeling better on my own."

"You were getting stronger, healing," Dr. Hector says. "Fatigue can be a factor in depression. But if you feel yourself sliding downward, give me a call. You're dealing with a lot here, both mentally, physically, and emotionally. A lot of this is experimental, so we don't really know all the possible side effects. Keep in touch."

"I will," I say.

• • •

It's great to be home recovering in my own room. (There were no bathtubs in the hospital and I've missed it.) School has started, but I still don't have an okay from the doctors to begin. The one I had from Dr. Tim has been voided by the new operations.

Jason texts to ask how I'm doing. **Better every day**, I reply. **Are you coming over?**

After football practice.

Jason has been bringing me homework and make-up assignments almost every day since I got home. He gets here close to six and leaves pretty quickly. Between football practice and school and caddying, he's busy.

He holds my left hand and kisses me lightly on the lips

sometimes, but he acts like he's scared I'll break. "I'm stronger than I was before," I tell him, "not more fragile."

"I know but . . . still."

"Still what?"

"It's not like we can exactly . . . make out . . ." he argues.

"Would you want to if we could?" I ask.

"Sure. Of course," he replies.

• • •

Even with all the homework I'm trying to stay on top of, it's been so hard to be cooped up, first in the hospital and now at home. I'm restless. I want to get on with my life, go out and do something.

I grab a blank marble composition pad to begin a list: Ways to get on with things.

1. Do PT exercises

2. Contact old friends I've neglected

3. Get strong in every way

I'm not exactly certain what number three entails, but I'm determined to do it.

• • •

Everything appears softer so early in the morning just after dawn. I ride my bike to the lake, grateful that I *can* ride it. I can't believe how quickly all this is happening. The chip in my brain is a miracle.

After I lock my bike against a tree, I shake out my hair. In just a few days that chip is giving me clear skin, strong nails, and killer hair. It's bouncy, shiny, thick, and grows like crazy. My hair is now really curly, which it never was before. I'd always wanted curly hair, so I love it.

The weather was cool for a while, but it's warm again. Hot, really, an Indian summer.

I'm still on medical leave from school. For now I'm free. Free of school, free of the hospitals. Free.

Unchaining one of our three kayaks is a chore since I lean heavily on my cane. I stagger as I pull it to the sloped muddy patch where we always launch the kayaks. The lifejacket and paddles are stored inside the kayak. As I pull on the life vest it strikes me that this is simply another bionic device, but one I've never thought much about before. I strap it on and I can float, even if I'm unconscious. I've always been a good swimmer and resented having to wear the vest, but now it's just one of many additions that bestows additional abilities on me.

Getting settled in the kayak's hull is the really tricky part. The little boat wobbles as I slide in on a muddy incline leading into the water, but I manage, pushing off against the rocks that border the property. Once afloat, I screw together both sides of the paddle.

I'm able to keep on my bionic arm. At the hospital Dr. Hector told me the controls are encapsulated inside a waterproof tube. Like everything else, it's the latest innovation in prosthetics. When I row for the first time, the kayak shoots wildly out into the water, spinning like a top. Catching my startled breath, I laugh, relieved that I haven't tipped.

This happens because my bionic right arm is *so* much stronger than my left arm. It takes nearly ten minutes of practice before I stop rowing in circles. Left, right, left, left, right . . . Eventually I get the hang of it, though, and head out to the center of the lake.

The morning breeze carries the smell of lake water and wraps me in a cloak of sensation. No other body of water can duplicate the smell of a living lake: marsh, wet rock, underwater plant life, lily pads, fish—all tumbled together to make the unique essence. I've always been aware of it, but not like this. Now it nearly overpowers me. Part of me feels strange to be back out here, like I was when I was in a coma. I keep catching myself expecting to wake up in the sterile white-and-gray room. But the other part of me wants to stay forever, listening, watching. It feels like comfort.

I see every glittering wing as dragonflies dart past. Schools of small silvery fish glide beneath my kayak, following the wispy clouds that drift across the sky.

I paddle along slowly, quietly, listening to the birds that haven't migrated, the ones who weather over. They've just come awake for the day, each delivering its distinct call (the whistle of the red-winged blackbird is my favorite) to tell the other birds that it has survived the night. It is still there. The territory it claimed days earlier still belongs to it. It has not disappeared during the night.

I haven't disappeared during the night, either.

So I row, and I grow stronger.

8

I start school nearly a month late, but I start. The kids at school are welcoming, holding doors, smiling, waving. Even kids I don't know offer to help me. I don't need their help, but I accept it anyway. It seems like the friendly thing to do.

"You sure have changed since that day you first left the hospital," Leanna says. She steps back to study me more closely. "Like, in a big way," she adds.

Nodding, I smile. I haven't seen or heard from Leanna for a while, but she's acting like we just talked yesterday. I guess it's her way of smoothing things over. It's not a bad strategy, really.

She's right. I've undergone some big changes. I don't look like a monster anymore. Honestly, I'm better looking now than before the accident. My cheeks have evened out and all the kayak paddling I've been doing has given me shoulders and biceps like never before. I've started docking the kayak on some rocks and swimming, which I also think shows. The parts of me that still have skin are tan from all my time in the sun, and with all the time I've been spending in the water, I don't think I've ever felt so relaxed and at peace in my body.

"Cool arm," a boy I don't know says as I head to class. He seems to mean it, too.

"Welcome back," says Coach Sanders, passing me in the hall. "You look great!"

I thank her, smiling.

My first class is Western Civilization II. Jason's in my class. There's no seat left near him so I take one in the back of the room. The teacher is new this year so she doesn't mention me being there as anything unusual. I'm happy about that. I want to ease back into school as normally as possible.

There was a note attached to my schedule telling me to meet Mr. Curtin during my next period, which is a study hall.

"Hi, Mira," he greets me. "You look good. How are you feeling?"

"It was rough at first, but I feel pretty good these days."

"Science is so amazing. Look at that arm . . . Wow!"

"It takes some getting used to," I say. "I love it, though."

"You're a trooper, Mira. You have all my admiration."

"Thank you," I say, genuinely touched. "Thanks."

"But listen, I have to talk to you about some not-so-good news." He has the essay I've written on *Frankenstein* in his hand. I wrote it right after I came out of the hospital the second time. It's the final test for my Advanced Placement English class. "This is an interesting piece of writing," he says.

"Interesting?" I ask nervously.

"You brought a unique perspective to the essay, and I'm guessing it's due to your recent experiences. I thought your idea that Dr. Frankenstein should have made the monster a bride and allowed them to have children was original."

Interesting. Unique. Original. He's picking his words carefully and my trouble-sensing antennae goes up. His apologetic expression is also a clue.

"I get where you're coming from. It's a bold idea, really."

"But?" I know the *but* is coming.

"The advanced placement scoring committee didn't see it as speaking to the central themes of the novel. Science versus nature. The dangers of playing God. You treated the creation of the monster as if it were a positive achievement. The monster was a murderer. He was a failed experiment, not a successful new type of creation."

"Okay, so Dr. Frankenstein's creation had a few glitches," I admit. "But still . . . think of it! To create a moving, thinking, talking person!" Standing, I spread my arms wide. "Look at me! I'm just a few parts away from being an artificial creation myself."

"That's not true," he protests.

"It's an exaggeration, I know. But science has caught up to Frankenstein. Well, almost, anyway," I say as I sit.

"I wrote the committee with similar thoughts. Sorry to say, though, they didn't go for it. They gave you a fail on your final test."

A fail!

"That means I don't get credit for the course, doesn't it?"

He nods. "Technically, it just means that you don't get college credit, but the English department here at Moon has always made passing the test a requirement for passing the course. Which leaves you an English language arts requirement short for graduation."

"You mean I won't graduate?"

"Not in May, unless you can join one of my senior elective classes if your study skills periods let you."

He hands me a schedule. Upon comparing it with my existing schedule I see that it does not, in any way, allow me to squeeze in another English class.

We look at each other for a moment. "Well, that sucks," I say. "All because they don't agree with my opinion?"

"They feel you've missed the point of the novel."

"Well, I feel they're still living in the eighteen hundreds."

This makes him smile. "I agree, but I couldn't sway them."

"Thanks for trying."

"Sorry. It's school policy."

"Couldn't they change it for a special situation like mine?"

"I can ask, but you've missed a lot of school, Mira. There's talk of having you graduate next year, anyway. It might be good to wait, to not put so much pressure on yourself while you're still adjusting. I'd love to have you in my class again in the fall.

Almost the moment I leave Mr. Curtin's class, I run into Taylor from my lacrosse team. "Mira!" she shouts shrilly, throwing her arms around me. Then she draws back. "Ew! It feels so weird to touch you, with that arm and all. You're a regular little robot girl now, aren't you?" All the while she's saying this she has a stiff smile on her face and her eyes sparkle. It's hard to tell if she's being insulting or just dumb. "I've missed you!"

"You have?" I say, not really knowing *what* to say.

"Of course, we all have! The team, I mean. We had a bad season last spring after you . . . left. We were all so upset. It's going to be hard without you this year, too."

"Hopefully I can play," I say.

She folds me in another rib-rattling hug. "You're so funny! Good to see you. I'd better get back to class. I'm out here on a bathroom pass. Bye!" I watch as she scurries down the hall.

Not such a great way to begin my big school comeback.

OCTOBER

Dr. Hector approves of my kayaking and thinks that continuing to swim on a schedule might be perfect PT. "Even though you have these powerful cable yarn muscles, you have to keep fit. All your organs and bodily systems are adjusting to these huge changes. It's critical that your body stays well oxygenated and that the cable muscles are challenged daily, and swimming in the lake was a great instinct on your part, but now that it's getting cold we have to find you a pool."

"The school has one," I tell him.

"Excellent."

So Dr. Hector writes a note and I receive special permission to swim laps after school and during my study halls.

I swim and swim and swim. It's almost as good as the lake, and nearly as comforting as soaking in the bathtub. I don't love the chlorine, but I can bear it. While swimming I can disappear from reality, lost in the underwater blur.

Dr. Hector has given me a few feet that can click on or off the titanium half leg. The foot I wear for the pool has a small flipper attached to it and rubber bottom to avoid slipping. Zack says I'm a metal mermaid, but the extra push it gives means I have to practice to avoid swimming in circles, just like I did with the kayak.

One day I'm stepping out of the pool when one of the gym teachers approaches me. I know her name is Mrs. Patrick, but I've never been in any of her gym classes.

"Ever think of joining the swim team?" she asks me. "I know you're just getting back into the swing of things," she continues.

"But I've been watching and you could be a competitive swimmer."

I point down to my swim leg. "This helps."

Folding her arms, Mrs. Patrick studies my foot. "Wow! That's amazing," she murmurs. "Is it difficult to swim with that prosthetic leg?"

"Just the opposite. The flipper actually provides a lot of forward propulsion." I shiver and go for my towel on the bench. Mrs. Patrick tells me to change and meet her back by the pool.

The locker room is empty, which I'm glad of. I need to remove my swimmer foot and change to my regular walking leg and foot. It makes me self-conscious when I have to change legs because the other girls all have me fixed in sidelong glances even though they don't blatantly stare. At first I tried to do it in a changing stall, but it's difficult balancing in such a narrow space.

I return wearing jeans and a long-sleeved T-shirt, which has become my uniform these days. As soon as I sit, Mrs. Patrick tells me that someone has dropped out of the swim team and she needs a replacement.

"You're such a strong swimmer," she says. "Would you want to join the team?"

I hesitate for a second, watching her face closely. I hope this isn't a pity thing. I can picture my guidance counselor, Ms. Trip, asking Mrs. Patrick to "get her *involved* in something." Could Mom have called and asked her to do it?

"I don't want anyone feeling sorry for me," I say. "I've never swum competitively before."

"This isn't about me doing you any favors. You'd be doing us the favor by filling in at the last minute. You tell me," she says. "Are you up to it?"

Strange as it might sound, the main thing that hurts right now is my artificial cheekbone. The entire ridge of my eye socket is still tender to the touch. Otherwise, I feel great. My mood is up, too, without the depression medications.

"I'd be willing to give it a try," I say.

• • •

The first thing I do is call Emma to tell her the news. "Can you believe I'll be on the swim team?"

"Maybe that's the change Madame Suza saw?" Emma says. "The number fifty-six."

I'd nearly forgotten about the palm reader. "What do you mean?"

"What if she saw you turning into a fish?"

"I'd say that's pretty unlikely," I reply.

Emma laughs at her own silliness. "Of course it is. You've already proven her right . . . so many changes. I wonder if you're done with the changes."

"I'd better be," I say. "I don't think I could stand any more of them."

"Oh, I know another change that's coming. You're getting back with Electric Storm!"

"No, I'm not!"

"If you're strong enough to swim, you're strong enough to play guitar and sing."

"Then I'll be right back where I started, with too much to do. Plus, I don't think I can sing anymore."

"Of course you can!"

"No, Emma, I've tried. Really. I can't."

Emma sighs and I sigh, too. "Have you tried since you got the new chip thing in your head?" Emma asks.

"Emma! Let's drop it, okay?"

"Okay," she says in a tone that really means: *I'll agree to stop talking, but you're wrong not to try again.*

"It's exciting about the swimming though, isn't it?" I say. I form a mental picture of myself getting in great shape by swimming competitively. By lacrosse season, who knows? That lacrosse scholarship might not be out of the question, even if it's delayed a little.

• • •

I start swim team practice today. The girls are standoffish at first, not rude, but not welcoming, either. I know one of the girls,

Elana, from Western Civ I last year. At least I have someone to talk to.

"None of us thought you could even walk," she tells me as we stand around the pool. "I was amazed when I heard you were joining the team."

I nod. "It *is* kind of mind-blowing."

Mrs. Patrick blows her whistle. "Into the pool. Warm up." I start with my favorite stroke, the butterfly. So much shoulder strength is required as I lunge forward out of the water. My shoulders are strongly developed from using the bionic arm and from all the rowing and swimming. That's probably why I'm good at the butterfly stroke.

Mrs. Patrick assesses each girl as she swims.

"Don't strain your neck when you turn to breathe. Roll your head," she tells a girl doing the freestyle crawl.

"The thumb should hit the water first," she says to another, who is doing the backstroke.

"So few girls are strong in the butterfly," Mrs. Patrick says to me when I'm out of the pool. "It takes a lot of upper body strength. You've got it, even with the prosthetic. I want to work on your freestyle, though. You could use some better breath control there."

. . .

That night I make supper for Zack because Mom is working late. More grilled cheese and soup. (But this time I remember to cut it on the diagonal, diner style.)

"Guess what swimming stroke the coach thinks I'm best at?" I say, sitting beside him at the table.

"I don't do guessing," he tells me between neat, tidy soup sips.

"The butterfly!"

Putting down his spoon, he casts a narrow-eyed look at me. "Is this a joke?"

"No, silly! I'm telling you the truth. Look!" Leaving the table, I demonstrate the upper part of the stroke. My arms scoop the air in big, round curves as I undulate my spine doing the best imitation I can.

"I see the wings, but that's not how butterflies fly," Zack says.

He proceeds to do his interpretation of a butterfly flying.

"No, like this!" I continue my stroke, which strikes me as being more like a dolphin breaching the waves than a butterfly flapping its wings, but I've staked my position and I feel bound to defend it.

"No! This is how," Zack insists. Even though Zack is often mystified by humor, he knows this is a game.

We circle the kitchen, still waving our arms and bobbing our heads, yelling.

"This way!"

"No, this way!"

Mom arrives home and walks in on this scene. She sinks into a chair, smiling. All three of us are smiling—and it feels so good to be happy.

. . .

Later that night, Jason and I have our usual FaceTime conversation. "I can't believe you joined swim team!" he cries, indignant.

"What's the problem?" I ask. "Who would think I'd even be able to swim, forget competitive swimming? I'd think you'd be happy for me. I can't believe this makes you mad," I say. Which is true. I assumed he'd be all, *"Good for you, Mira!"*

"All this time I've waited for you to get better. Now that you're better—or better than better—super, or whatever you are—you're too busy for me again. It's going to be the same old thing, just like before the accident."

"I have a right to a life! The doctors want me swimming, to help support my prosthetics. And I need to be able to hang out with friends—you see the guys on your team all the time! Do you think you should be the only thing in my life? It's not just me. All summer you were caddying and now you have football. I don't give you a hard time about it."

His face gets red and he rolls his eyes as frustration overpowers his language skills. I don't regret my words, though. I've finally expressed the thing that has bothered me about Jason the whole time we've been together. No matter what I do, if it doesn't involve him, it hurts his feelings.

"You totally don't get it!" Jason says.

He's right about that!

Are we breaking up or just having a fight?

"Do you want to get out of this . . . this . . . relationship?" I ask. There. I've released the dreaded question. I imagine it hanging in a puff of small black clouds. Unrecoverable.

"Do you?" he asks. Did I hear a trace of hopefulness in the question? I think I did.

The reality crashes in on me all at once. He's *glad* we have a reason to argue. He wants an *excuse* to break up.

"I asked you first," I say, even though I know it's about the most childish thing in the world.

Jason sighs. "I just wish you had thought of me before you went and joined swim team."

I can't believe that after all I've been through, how changed I am in every way, I'm still going round and round with Jason on this same old issue. It just seems too ridiculous.

"Do you want me to quit the team?" I ask.

His face suddenly becomes softer. "We'd have more time to be together." He's sulking but congenial.

He thinks he's gotten his way.

Has he?

Would I rather swim or spend more time with Jason?

"I think it's time for us to . . ." My voice breaks. I can't! "Let's just think about it."

. . .

My first swim meet is an invitational at River Crest High School. I'm not sure if I should wear my swim leg. I've been wearing it at practice. "Go ahead," Mrs. Patrick says. "Let's see if anyone objects."

Wearing my tank suit at my own school didn't bother me much. Over the course of more than three years there, the school has come to be like a second home, and I know pretty much all the seniors and juniors. Here at River Crest, though, I feel uncomfortably exposed. I catch lots of people staring. Am I some kind of freak show to them? The coach of the other team listens to her team captain, who keeps glancing at me.

The pool shimmers like a crystal blue oasis of calm amidst the chaos of chatting friends and parents in the bleachers, coaches giving last-minute instructions, and assistants scurrying around with towels, caps, timers, and whistles. The swimmers stretch, limbering their muscles. Bending, I grasp my fake swimmer's foot with my good hand and real toes with my prosthetic hand.

Slowly, I inhale as deeply as I can in an effort to expand my lungs before blowing out the air.

The first event is freestyle, and I'm competing. With my cap and goggles on, I line up with the other swimmers. I take my place on the dive boards in front of our designated lane. The chlorine smell is nearly overwhelming.

When the buzzer sounds, I do my best race dive into the pool. The cheering of our teammates and of those in the bleachers is muffled by the water. I come to the surface and realize that I'm ahead of the other swimmers.

I am nothing but speed and motion in the water. When I make it to the other side, I tap the ledge, feeling its cool smoothness with my bionic hand. I curl into an underwater flip turn and shoot back. I'm now side by side with one of the River Crest swimmers who has sped up suddenly. We seem to slap the pool's edge at the same moment, but the timers say she beats me by a second.

"Nice job, Mira!" Elana says, throwing me a towel as I return to my teammates.

"Way to go!" cries another. The other girls clap and cheer.

Wrapped in a towel, I sit on the bench with my teammates watching the next bunch of competitions, clapping along and shouting encouragement. I'd forgotten how much I like being part of a team, training together, supporting each other. It feels like old times on the lacrosse team.

The next time I'm up is for the butterfly. I think the butterfly stroke is more difficult than freestyle, but Mrs. Patrick says I'm better at it than most, probably because of all the PT. My arm, though it's so strong, is heavier than a natural arm. In practice, I've been working hard not to let it steer me into the lane ropes.

I wait on my dive board, bending to touch the edge, getting ready to dive. I'm determined to do my best, even though I don't expect much. When the buzzer sounds, I blast off from the side, arms circling. I can't tell if I'm first, last, or somewhere in the middle. I'm just swimming with all I've got. I get to one side, shoot back, and slap the side of the pool when I arrive. The timer clicks her stopwatch. Standing in front of my lane, she holds it in the air.

I've won first place in butterfly!

My teammates go crazy, cheering and thumping my back. "Great work!" Mrs. Patrick says.

"You were ahead the whole time," Elana tells me.

I notice that the River Crest coach is talking to Mrs. Patrick, but I don't think much of it until they approach me. They look serious. Mrs. Patrick beckons for me to join them. "There's been a complaint, Mira. About you."

"None of the other girls have the advantage of flippers," the River Crest coach says.

"They have the *advantage* of fully functional limbs," Mrs. Patrick points out.

"Even so," the River Crest coach insists. "There are handicapped teams for persons with special needs." She turns to me, speaking as if I'm five. "Would you prefer something like that, dear?"

I force a smile. "No. I'd like to stay with this team."

I'd like to push her into the pool, is what I'd like to do.

"Next time I'll wear my walking foot. Okay if I lock it into pointed-toe position for swimming?"

Her face looks stiff. This is clearly making her very uncomfortable. "Of course. That would be fine."

• • •

I want to call Jason to tell him about my first competition, but I don't feel I can, since he hates the swim team. Just like he hated Electric Storm. Just like he hates me doing anything that means I'm not at his beck and call, really.

Mom takes me out for ice cream with Zack. "Now you're a butterfly!" Zack states as he licks his vanilla cone. (Vanilla is the only flavor he'll eat.) "I wonder if the doctors will give you wings next? You should ask them."

"She should ask for fins," Mom says.

"No," Zack disagrees. "She's already got fins."

"Yes, but I'm not allowed to wear them. They think it makes me better than all the other swimmers."

"You are better than all the others," Zack says. "They're just going to have to get used to it."

9

Invitational swim meet number two is here at our school. I use my walking foot, taking it out of walking position and locking it into a pointed toe at the edge of the pool.

At the end I place first in butterfly *and* freestyle. Second in backstroke.

. . .

Today, I'm called to the office. The local news station wants to interview me. They're in the gym because the school secretary has made them wait until I have a study period.

When I walk in, there's a young woman reporter, who's pretty with dark hair, and an older man with a video camera. We sit on some folding chairs to the side of the basketball court.

"How does it feel to make such a comeback after your terrible accident?" the reporter asks. She wears that *fake sincere* expression a lot of TV reporters use.

"Great, of course." *No, it feels terrible. I wish I were still immobilized in a hospital bed.* Is this the best question she can come up with?

"Who are your heroes?

I speak before I even think. "The people who took care of me in the hospital, the doctors, the nurses, the therapists. The researchers and scientists who come up with all this cool stuff." As I speak, I raise my bionic arm and hand. "My mom, too."

"Your mother?" the reporter questions.

I nod. "Definitely! She keeps me going."

"What advice do you have for young people struggling with handicaps?"

"It's hard. Don't give up. Science is getting better every day."

"What have you learned from this experience?"

What *have* I learned? I don't know.

So I don't answer. "Swim team is a great experience," I say. "I'm grateful to have it in my life." This much is true.

The reporter seems not to notice that I haven't answered, and nods with a smile.

I smile back—with equal sincerity.

• • •

After the interview, I head to Jason's locker. It's the end of my study hall and his lunch. Since the interview finished up before end of period, I figure I'll wait there to surprise him. When I turn the corner, I stop. Taylor is at his locker. They're laughing and smiling at each other.

The body language is all there. This is a *thing*. They're so obviously into each other.

I duck back into the corner so they can't see me.

How do I feel? What does this mean to me?

But then he kisses her.

And all my calm evaporates as tears run down my face. Everything I've suspected is true. I feel so betrayed and I miss him already.

Should I go out there and make a scene?

I can't! It's just not me. Instead, head down, I hurry back toward the nearest girl's room, my face swollen with tears.

• • •

LOCAL TEEN SWIM STAR TURNS TRAGEDY TO TRIUMPH.

I'm front-page news—at least in my local paper. They've taken the TV interview and printed it with my photo from last week's swim meet. Tonight I'll be on the Channel 12 news.

Mom reads the paper at the kitchen table, beaming with pride. She hugs me and I hug back, making a special effort to be gentle, not to leave her struggling for air.

Easing away I see her eyes sparkle with tears. "We've been so blessed, so lucky," she says. "And you deserve all of it. You've worked so hard."

It's the first time anyone has acknowledged all the hours I've spent doing my PT exercises and exercising on my own. It's so nice to be acknowledged as a person who's trying, and not just a patient or an experiment. "Thanks, Mom," I say as she leaves.

It's too cold now to keep kayaking at the lake in the mornings, but I'm running instead, doing everything I can think of to master this new body. Even though the cable yarn muscles and the chip in my head have amplified my strength incredibly, it all requires a new kind of balance and coordination I have to work at.

Dr. Hector says it's the chip that gives me so much energy.

I feel it most when I swim. For the first time in my life, I'm not struggling to be good enough, like I did with lacrosse, not worrying about slipping into the number two or even three position, not anxious about losing all that I've worked for at any moment.

Everything is coming naturally to me. I'm not sweating it.

It dawns on me that up until now I've lived my life in a constant state of low-level anxiety. How sad is that? It's so pathetic to constantly believe I'm not good enough, that the positive occurrences in my life are no more than patches of random luck. I didn't even realize I was feeling that way, but it's clear to me now that I was.

Jason calls. "Hi, babe," he begins. Babe! How can he call me that after what I saw in the school hall yesterday? He must know something's wrong. I didn't pick up his FaceTime call last night.

I've ignored all his texts. Shouldn't that throw up a few warning signals for him? Judging from his cheery tone, it doesn't seem to have.

"Saw the story in the paper. Cool. Congratulations," he says.

"Saw you in the hall with Taylor. Cool. Congratulations," I say, feeling very superior and clever.

"What?" He sounds genuinely surprised.

"Do you think I'm stupid? How long has it been going on?"

He clears his throat.

I decide not to be so mean. "It's all right, Jason," I say more kindly. "I know she likes you, and I haven't exactly been around."

"I didn't want to tell you right now. I mean, you've been through so much already."

"It's okay," I say. "Really. I'll see you sometime, I guess."

I hang up and sit down, trying to absorb what's just happened. Jason and I are no longer together. Panic rises as I consider this: I'm not the same girl I used to be. That girl was pretty likely to find a new boyfriend after a while. But who will want to date this new me—Bionic Girl?

Zack comes in holding a new book. He sprawls on the floor and proceeds to page through it, pausing to study the color photos. "No butterflies?" I ask.

"I'll always love butterflies," he says, looking up from his book, "but I've moved on to beetles. You look weird. Is something wrong?"

"Jason and I just broke up."

"Good," he says evenly. "I never liked him."

. . .

Later that day I get another call on the home main line. I don't recognize the number, but I pick up.

"I'm looking for Mira Rains." It's a network TV news show. They saw me on Channel 12 and want to do a quick human-interest piece on me and Dr. Hector to show at the end of the news. Will I do it? They'll need Mom's permission. I tell them I'll have Mom call them back.

Network news! Me!

Joy melts into panic. Me . . . on TV. Not the local station . . . network TV!

"Mira, what's wrong?" Mom asks, coming into the living room. "You're trembling."

I tell her what just happened and show her the contact name and phone number I've typed into the notes app on my phone. "This is exciting," she says, though her voice is more cautious than excited. "Are you interested in doing this?"

"Yes. Just nervous."

"Are you sure? When I walked in you looked like you were about to faint."

"Nervous, like I said." An upsetting thought comes to me. "You don't think it could be a prank, do you?" I ask nervously.

"I'll know when I call back," she says. Putting the phone on speaker so I can hear, she calls. I'm relieved of worry when the call goes directly to a voice menu greeting the caller and going directly to a list of extensions. She talks to someone who wants to see us the next day at seven o'clock in the morning in their office in Manhattan.

"Can I skip school?" I ask, hoping she'll agree.

"For something this big . . . yes," she says.

That night I can't fall asleep. I'm so nervous. At least my anxiety takes my mind off Jason.

10

When we get to the TV studio, Dr. Hector is already in the office with the reporter Jane Evans. I've seen her a million times on TV and am surprised that she's so much shorter and thinner than she appears on screen.

"You look great, kiddo." Dr. Hector greets me with a hug. Shaking Mom's hand, he asks if I've been doing my PT and she assures him that I have. "I know you're swimming. I saw it on the news. Good stuff!"

Jane Evans tells us that our piece will be only three minutes long, but they'll shoot for about a half hour to make sure they have the best footage. "Can you stay for about two hours?" she asks. "You need to go through makeup and hair, and we'll take some press photos as well."

I feel like I'm in a dream—a great dream.

"You have a great look," the studio hairdresser says as she scrunches my curls, making them even curlier, while blow-drying my hair. "You should model."

"With this arm?" I say with a laugh.

"Why not? It makes you stand out from the rest. It's like your trademark."

Modeling almost seems possible after the hair and makeup people are done with me. I barely recognize myself, but in a good way. My curls are wildly thick. They give me a short denim dress and ankle booties. Jane Evans pops her head into the room. "Adorable!" she says. "Can you roll up the sleeves on that cute dress? We want to see your amazing arm. Is that okay?"

"Fine," I agree, pushing up my sleeves.

Like Jane Evans, the set is way smaller than it appears on TV. It's absolutely tiny! But there's room for three chairs and even a narrow coffee table. Jane and Dr. Hector are already seated when I arrive. Mom is on a couch off to the side. She gives a thumbs-up when she sees me. I smile and take a deep breath to steady my nerves.

"Just be natural," Jane instructs us as the camerapeople position themselves. "We can always reshoot anything you want to change, so don't worry."

Dr. Hector smiles at me. "Ready, kiddo? This is our big TV debut."

"I'm ready if you are," I reply.

"Good. Let's do this thing."

When we begin, a narrator in a booth up near the ceiling

tells about how I was "snatched from the jaws of death after a hideous collision with a fuel tanker and an SUV last April."

Jane then asks Dr. Hector how he accounts for my "astounding recovery."

Dr. Hector explains that the copper implant in my head makes it all possible. "The chip communicates wirelessly with all of Miranda's body systems, encouraging them to work at their optimum capacity," he says. "The chip, in combination with her state-of-the-art prosthetics and the cable yarn muscle replacement, not only returns her to her former healthy self, but, in fact, enhances her physical performance beyond what she was previously capable of doing."

"Dr. Hector," Jane says, turning to him and tilting her head just so. "Do you foresee a day when healthy people will seek these artificial limbs, cable muscles, and chip implants, not to recover but to improve their bodies?"

"Yes, it's happening already. What our study is really about, however, is making a better life for people who have tragically lost limbs either through war, accidents, or disease."

"Mira, are you satisfied with the quality of life you have now?"

"I am," I say honestly. "It wasn't easy getting to this point, but in so many ways I'm even stronger now than I was."

"Let me tell you," Dr. Hector cuts in, "this kid is a champion.

She has endured so much pain, so many operations, but she keeps her chin up and even jokes around. Everyone at the hospital was crazy about her. She really was at the brink of death last April, but look at her now."

"She's a real role model for all of us," Jane agrees.

I sure hope I'm not blushing or that my smile isn't too wide, because all this praise sure feels great.

Jane Evans asks us some more questions before the narrator up in the booth ends by saying, "Thanks to cutting-edge technology, Miranda Rains, science's first bionic girl, is better than all right—she's super!"

• • •

Emma and I sit on the floor in front of the TV set. Mom and Zack are on the couch behind us. At the end of the nightly news, Emma and I shriek with anticipation as the camera starts showing photos of me as a child. "Did you give them those?" I ask Mom, who nods. The narrator from the booth speaks over the photos in a voice-over. "Seventeen-year-old Miranda Rains, who was snatched from the jaws of death after a hideous collision with a fuel tanker and an SUV last April . . ."

Then Jane Evans comes on and the interview part begins. "You look so cute!" Emma says. "I love that dress!"

"I had to give it back," I tell her sadly.

"You should get one just like it."

My voice sounds sort of high-pitched, probably because of my nervousness, but otherwise I'm pretty happy with the way I appear. I think I did well.

As the credits roll, the house phone begins to ring. First it's my aunt, and then Emma's parents call to say how wonderful I looked and how impressive they thought Dr. Hector was. Leanna and Elana call my phone, one after the other, to congratulate me.

I see Niles is trying to break through, so I cut the call with Elana short. "Man, you were awesome! Amazing! You were like a professional actress."

My smile is stretched across my face. I'm beaming. "I was not, but thanks."

"You were so great. The guys and I were practicing, but we stopped to watch you. We're all at Matt's house now. They all want to talk to you. Here . . ." Niles passes the phone to Tom, and then Matt.

"Hey, you're a famous person now, and we know you," Tom jokes.

"I am not famous," I say.

Then Matt sounds more serious. "Mira, I've never said this but . . . I was driving that day, and I'm like, you know . . . sorry. Really sorry."

"It was an accident, Matt. I don't blame you."

"I blame me."

"Well, don't," I say.

I'm only off the phone for a moment when the house phone rings from a number I don't recognize. I pick up and an unfamiliar voice speaks. "Can I speak to Mira Rains?"

"That's me. Who's calling?"

"My name is Sylvia Marcus and I represent Snap Girl Cosmetics. We just saw you on TV and we believe you're just the kind of fresh young face we're looking for. We would like to talk to you about possibly endorsing Snap Girl."

"Is this for real?" I ask, once more suspicious of a prank.

Sylvia Marcus laughs. "I assure you this is a genuine offer. We'd pay for your endorsement, of course."

I'm stunned, still a little suspicious that it's not real.

We make an appointment to meet at her office in New York City. Mom comes in and I tell her. She's excited. "This is a whole new beginning for you," she says.

11

Sylvia Marcus comes out to the lobby to greet Mom and me. Her walk is so smooth she seems to glide. Her honey-blond hair shines and her voice is silky as she clasps my bionic hand. "I can't tell you how moved I was by your story. I called our head of marketing immediately from my apartment. I told him, 'I have found our Snap Girl.' I am so delighted to meet you."

She turns to Mom. "Thrilled to meet the heroic mother of this inspiring survivor."

When we get to Sylvia Marcus's spacious office, we meet a lawyer with a stack of papers for Mom to read. "These are just preliminary one-time-only contracts and releases," she says. "If the first commercial goes well and all parties are in agreement, we'll sign a more permanent deal."

"I'd like to read these over before I sign anything," Mom replies.

"Why don't you take Mrs. Rains to your office so you can answer any questions she might have, while I show Mira around," Sylvia Marcus suggests to the lawyer.

The photography studio is filled with glamorous-looking photographers and models. Sylvia Marcus shows me their complete line of Snap Girl makeup and hair products.

"You simply have that wholesome prettiness we've been searching for," she tells me. "Your face says old-fashioned American beauty, but your arm and leg tell your story of strength and grit. The arm especially says that you're the girl of tomorrow."

"Wow," I say quietly, not really sure how to respond to all this.

"Absolutely," she says. "You have one foot in the past and the other in the future. And that's what Snap Girl is all about."

Later that afternoon, Mom and I drive back home. I feel strangely drained of energy, especially considering that I haven't done very much. It must be from seeing so many new people and places. I worry that if I become the Snap Girl representative, I won't even know what I'm talking about.

"You're quiet," Mom comments.

"I'm just thinking. You know, I've never really worn a lot of makeup. I don't even know what brand the lip gloss in my bag is."

"No one thinks the actors who make these commercials mean what they say," she assures me. "Everyone knows you're being paid to speak the lines that are given to you. It's just a commercial. Do you think all those celebrities in magazine ads really wear the drugstore makeup brands they're modeling for?"

I guess she's right. I've never stopped to think about it before this. "But isn't it still lying?" I say.

"You could think of it as playing a part in a movie. Everyone knows the actors are just speaking lines."

"That's true, but if you *endorse* something isn't that lie saying you use the product and like it?"

"I have an idea," Mom says. "I'm going to call our lawyer to look over these papers. Meanwhile, they gave you a bag of products. Why don't you go home and use them. Maybe you'll like them."

"Good idea," I say. I sure hope I like them because I'd love to be the face of Snap Girl.

• • •

I'm not sure that I *love* Snap Girl makeup and hair products. They're all right. No big deal. But I make sure to use them and wear the makeup every day. This way I won't have any conflict in my head when I shoot my first commercial. It's a good thing that I get more made up and look more presentable than usual, because I've become sort of a celeb around school.

I don't know whether it's because of my TV appearances on the news shows or because word has gotten around that I'm sort of the new swim champ. The swim invitationals, which usually only have a smattering of parents in the audience, are now completely packed with people wanting to see—let's face it—me.

I win almost every competition in every category. To make things more fair, I offer to use no fake leg at all, letting my leg end at the stump of my knee. It only *reduces* my time, but I still win. I wonder, though, if I'm pushing a little too hard. At the last practice I swam without my prosthetic and my half leg cramped so painfully that I gasped in pain and swallowed a mouthful of water. Luckily, I was able to pull myself out of the pool, coughing. As I sat rubbing my leg and taking deep breaths, Mrs. Patrick came to my side, concerned. She told me to skip the next practice to rest. I told her I didn't need to. I don't want her thinking I can't keep up with the schedule.

The cramping didn't happen again and, mostly, I win and win and win. This makes me extremely popular with my teammates.

Tonight, Elana invites me to a party at her mini mansion, which is in a development of other mini mansions. I see Niles across the room talking to some guys I don't know. He's still leaning heavily on that cane. Why isn't he getting better?

"Wow! Mira!" he says when I approach. "You look awesome."

"Thanks." I want to ask if he's gotten taller since I last saw him. Even though he's bent from leaning on the cane, he looks like he's grown. I don't want to embarrass him by asking. "You look good, too," I say.

He blushes. "Thanks."

His friends drift away, leaving us alone.

"Are you still using the 3-D printer at school?" I ask.

"I'm in that lab every second I get," he replies, nodding. "It's the coolest thing, Mira."

I'm wearing tights under a blue wool dress that comes just below my knee, with over-the-knee boots. When I'm dressed like this you can hardly tell there's anything different with my legs at all. But I tap my right knee. "This knee was made with a 3-D printer," I tell him.

Niles drops onto the couch beside me. "Can I touch it?"

I nod.

He puts his hand on my knee. It's unexpectedly thrilling.

"Feels just like a real knee," he remarks, looking up at me.

"I know," I say, sitting beside him.

"The printer is unbelievable," Niles says. "I've built a whole model city of the future just by entering my designs into the computer. If I ever run out of picks for my guitar, I just print out more of them."

The mention of guitar picks reminds me of Electric Storm. "Any interesting gigs lately?"

"Things have kind of trailed off," he says. "We just don't sound as good without you."

I kiss him playfully on the cheek with an exaggerated *mwah* sound. "You say the sweetest things," I joke.

"I mean it. You have to come back."

"What is that smell?" I ask. He's wearing something that smells woodsy. A cologne or soap? "It's nice."

"I must be sweating," he says with a smile. "I exude wood-land freshness."

I arch my eyebrow skeptically.

"That's my story and I'm sticking to it. But returning to the subject of Electric Storm . . . How about giving it another try?"

"You heard me last time," I remind him. "My voice sucked and I couldn't remember the words."

"Nuh-uh," Niles says. "You can't fool me. I saw your story on TV, remember? You've had work done since then. I can hear it just talking to you now. Your voice is a lot stronger. A lot! It sounds fuller."

I *have* sort of noticed it.

For a moment I consider the offer. I've missed the band. I decide it's not the best idea, though. "If I'm going to play lacrosse this season, I'd better stay focused on that. Plus, swim team. The Fordham lacrosse scout is very interested, and if I play as well as I've been swimming, I'm sure to score that scholarship."

"Don't you make enough from that commercial?"

"Not enough for four years of college. They're not telling me how long it will run, either. As soon as it stops the payments stop."

"They'll make another," Niles says.

"Maybe, maybe not."

"They will," he assures me.

A song we both like comes on. "Want to dance?" Niles asks.

"Can you," I ask, "with your cane and all?"

"I can bob around," he says, and he begins to move. I join him and it's almost like before, when we danced around together on the stage, as though the last seven months haven't happened.

At least, it's like that for me. I'm perfectly balanced. I have to consciously control the spring in my step. It's strangely ironic that Niles, who didn't seem to be hurt all that badly, can only sway while I, who was smashed into mashed potatoes, am doing so well.

Next, we dance to a slow song. He leans on his cane and we sway in place. He's definitely grown because I can now rest my head against his shoulder, and I'm even a little taller than I was, since the cable muscles give me perfect posture.

Thinking about the cable muscles suddenly worries me. I lift my head and pull back. "Niles, is it strange touching me?"

"Strange?"

"Do I feel . . . artificial?"

"You feel strong," he says continuing to hold me and sway to the music.

"Weird strong?" I question.

"No. Beautiful strong."

I smile into his eyes. "Really?"

"Definitely." His eyes shine back at me for a moment and he pulls me a little closer.

Something about him is different. "Your eyes look greener," I say.

"They've gotten worse, so I have contacts now," he says, continuing to dance. "Tinted contacts."

"I didn't know you were so vain," I tease.

He shrugs it off. "Why not?"

I lay my head on his shoulder. I'm not thinking about anything. This isn't like being onstage together. I've never danced close with Niles before. It feels nice.

• • •

There's a notice that I've overlooked on the sports bulletin board—a meeting this afternoon of the lacrosse team. It's to discuss the upcoming year, talk about tryouts, and figure out who will be playing what positions. It will make me a half hour late for swim practice, so I go to ask Mrs. Patrick if that's all right.

Mrs. Patrick is in the gym office, reading something at her desk. My approach startles her. "Mira, hi. I'm glad you're here. I need to talk to you."

"Is something wrong?" I drop into a chair across from her.

"I've received a letter from the High School Athletic Association. It's about you."

"Me?"

"It seems that some of the local swim coaches have written to them complaining that your prosthetics give you an unfair advantage."

"I took off my swim leg," I say. "Should I take off my arm?"

Mrs. Patrick taps her forehead. "It's the chip."

"The chip," I echo her.

"And the cable yarn muscle," she adds. "That TV spot got you a lot of attention, but it also told them about all your surgeries, so they know what sort of advantages you have."

"Isn't it against the law to keep a person with disabilities from playing?" I know I read that somewhere.

Sighing, she sits back in her chair. "You know this is different. You're not *dis*abled. You're *extra*-abled."

"Does this mean I can't compete?" I ask.

"They're going to form a committee to review your case," Mrs. Patrick tells me.

"How long will that take?"

"They don't say. Until they come to a decision, you can't compete."

Even though I feel like crying, the tears don't spring forward like they used to. It's just one of my many improvements, I suppose.

"I'm sorry, Mira," Mrs. Patrick says. "Are you all right?"

"Does this mean I can't play lacrosse, either?"

"I'm afraid it does. However, I could use an assistant swim coach," she says.

"Thanks, but I have to swim or play lacrosse if I'm going to get a college scholarship. They care about the athletes, not assistant coaches."

"I know. I'm sorry."

Hot anger rises within me. The schools won't let me compete in any of the fields that will allow me to win scholarships to continue my schooling—how does that make sense? If I can't use school sports to my advantage, then why do I even need to stay in school? All of a sudden, I can't stand the idea of being here another second. "Who do I inform that I'm dropping out?"

"You don't want to do that, Mira."

"Yes, I do."

"You've been through a lot. Why don't you think about it? There's always community college."

"I don't want to go to community college."

"I went."

I don't want to be rude, but she's not me. Community college isn't what I had in mind for myself. I was so sure I could earn a lacrosse scholarship.

"You're just angry right now, Mira. Wait until you cool down."

"Thanks, anyway, Mrs. Patrick," I say as I leave.

At the main office I ask for a form to drop out of school, and fill it out in the parking lot, forging Mom's signature. Leaving it in the office in-box, I collect everything from my locker.

When I'm outside, I see that Emma has called me. I don't call her back. I'm not in the mood to talk to anyone.

Once I'm home, I begin my shower-and-bath ritual, washing my hair, drying off, filling the tub, and curling into the hot water. I'm so upset, though, not even warm running water can calm me down.

Why should I even finish school? I'm not the girl I once was. I'm about to be the "New Face of Snap Girl Cosmetics." Mom's lawyer told her it was okay to sign the contracts and releases. I'm quitting school!

• • •

That night I tell Mom I want to drop out. You'd think I told her I want to move to Antarctica—or the moon! "Absolutely not!" she cries looking shaken.

"I'll take the GED!"

"It's not the same as graduating," she says. "What about college?"

"I thought I needed a scholarship. I'm not getting one now."

"You can go to community college."

"What good is two years of college going to do me if I can't afford to finish?"

"It will give me two years to save."

"Come on, Mom! You can barely pay the bills each month as it is. How are you going to save? I'll work at the diner full time."

Zack comes into the room while we argue about this, going around in circles on the subject. We're so involved that we barely notice him until he shouts. "Stop!" His hands are over his ears. He scrunches his eyes shut. "Stop!"

Obeying his command, we stare at him, surprised by the outburst.

"If Mira doesn't want to go to school, she shouldn't have to," he tells Mom.

"Why not?" Mom asks him gently, patiently.

"Mira is special now. She's not like the other kids. I know what it's like."

"You do?" Mom questions.

"Yes. I'm special, too, so I know." Mom strokes his hair affectionately.

"It's great to be special," Mom says, "but you also have to learn how to live in the regular world with other people."

"No," Zack disagrees. "We're in our own worlds. It's better there."

"It's time for you to go take a bath and get ready for bed," Mom tells Zack. "Mira and I have to talk privately." Once he's upstairs she turns her attention back to me. "Is that what you really want to be—a full-time diner waitress?" Mom asks, sounding defeated.

"I don't know what I want to be. I just want a job until the Snap Girl commercial comes through. I've already called Carl, and he's agreed to put me on an afternoon shift. Since I worked there part time before the accident, he doesn't have to train me."

"Why are you doing this, Mira?"

"I don't fit in at school anymore. I'm not going to graduate with my class, anyway. They won't let me play sports because they say I have an unfair advantage. Most likely Snap Girl will want me to do something for them and I'll have to be more available, anyway."

Mom sits at the table and lets her head drop into her hands. "All right."

Standing, I hug her. "You'll see this is the right thing. The diner is just temporary. The Snap Girl thing is going to work."

I get into bed, my head buzzing from the day. I'm

overstimulated, the way kids get on Halloween when they've had too much candy.

My imagination goes wild, playing out in my mind a little drama in which I really tell off those idiots who failed my essay. In it I toss my fake arm at them and tell them to get real. It's a new world. My arm comes to life on its own and starts chasing them around. I go through this scenario a few times, because it makes me feel good.

I imagine what I would do if I didn't have school everyday. At first I think of all the things I've always wanted to do. Skydive. Surf. Perform in a band.

Thinking of that makes me want to see what's going on with Electric Storm, so I take my phone from my nightstand and go to the website Matt put up for us. It's pretty good, with cool graphics, a photo gallery, and videos. I check out a video of their latest gig. Matt's right. He's not a great vocalist. Niles, though, has written a new song. It's about a sorceress in a forest who is there some of the time, and other times she disappears. Though he doesn't usually sing, Matt and he sing this one together. I notice that he leans on his grandfather's cane, which has a strange troll-ish man at the head. He has a quirky, low, throaty voice. It works, at least on this song.

Niles is a good guy.

12

A full-length mirror hangs on the back of my bedroom door. I'm about to go to bed, so I wear the tank top and shorts that I sleep in. Rotating to get a full look, I stop to check over my shoulder for a rear view.

I am *all* muscle.

No kidding. Anyone would think that I spend all day lifting heavy weights and training, though I don't. Someone else would start to lose muscle tone, get flabby. I become more muscular by the day, but not in a bulky, bodybuilder way. I'm a little cut, though more than that, I'm just completely solid.

"Your body is adjusting to the chip beautifully," Dr. Hector tells me at my next visit. "You're going to start to see changes as your body begins working at optimal performance."

"Starts?" I question. "You mean this is only the beginning?"

"It is."

"What kind of changes?" I ask, worried.

"*You* tell *me* at your next visit. I don't want to put ideas in your mind. How's your memory these days?"

"Great!" I report.

"Let's see." He holds up a card on which a long string of

random numbers are printed. In about sixty seconds, he puts it down. "How many numbers can you remember?"

I recite them back, forty in all.

"That's amazing!" he says quietly. "You remembered every number correctly."

"Maybe optimal performance has already set in," I suggest.

"It looks that way," he agrees. He pulls out some pictures of my brain that were taken in the MRI. "See this fuzzy area here," he says showing an area of my brain that looks like cottage cheese. "That was your brain right after the accident. There are areas of damage, especially here." He indicates one section that looks darker than the bits around it. He turns over a different scan. "This is from your most recent MRI."

"Colorful," I observe.

"You bet it is! Your brain neurons are blinking on all circuits. Your brain is not merely as good as it once was, it's much better."

This proves to me that I don't need school anymore. I've made the right decision.

NOVEMBER

"Funny to run into you here," I tell Niles. We lean against the railing of the diner's handicapped ramp. He's perched on the top rung, his cane balanced against it. I'm on my fifteen-minute break and I saw Niles approach across the parking lot.

The afternoon's cold rain has subsided, but everything is still wet, puddles everywhere. Everyone has started wearing coats and scarves, but I'm just fine in a sweater because I'm not bothered by the cold these days.

"Not all that coincidental," he says. He looks down and away for a moment, but when he returns to me, his eyes are playful. "I heard you were working here."

"From who?"

"Elana."

She called me the day I left school and I'd told her I hoped to get a job here. She called several times after that, but I never answered her back. It seems easier to cut ties with the past. I'm not that person anymore.

Even so, I am glad to see Niles.

He looks different to me than the last time. My vision keeps advancing. It's becoming some version of ultra HDTV. Every strand of his hair shifts softly, tossed gently by the wet breeze. He's lost weight, which gives him an animal sharpness I've never noticed before. It makes him look older.

"I didn't just come to see you. I was buying some new strings for my guitar," he says.

"You couldn't 3-D print up some new ones?" I ask, only half kidding.

He smiles. "There's probably a way to do it, but I haven't figured it out. There's a music store place down the block," he says. "I went there to get the strings. Then I saw the diner and decided to drop in for a veggie burger. I heard they were good here and I'm trying to go vegetarian."

"Good for you," I say.

But I hope he's lying. I wish that he had come to see me, and that the veggie burger and guitar strings were an excuse.

Niles shifts from one leg to the other, as if deciding what to say next.

"How much break do you have left?" Niles asks.

"It was over three minutes ago."

"Then we'd better get inside."

"Oh, they'll never fire me," I say.

"Is that so?" he asks, amused. "And why is that?"

"Because I'm probably the greatest server this place has ever seen," I tell him. I grin, but it's the truth. "I can sprint across the entire diner in seconds. I can carry ten fully loaded plates, five balanced on each arm. I never forget an order—don't even have to write it down. I never complain that my feet hurt, because they never do. And last night I even strong-armed a drunken idiot customer and escorted him out the door."

"Wow!"

I'm bragging, but it's hard to stop when Niles is shooting me an admiring look like he is now.

"He'd been bothering Karen, one of the other waitstaff, and I just grabbed his shoulders and walked him right on out. The shocked expressions all around me were hilarious. I even got applause."

Niles smiles. "So you're a waitperson and a bouncer all in one."

My break is over, though, and despite my confidence I need to get back. "Come in and have that veggie burger," I suggest. "They're good here, especially with double cheese."

"Sounds great."

We smile at each other as though there's suddenly something shared between us, even though I can't name it. I push off the railing to go inside, but Niles grabs my arm lightly. "Why don't you come back and sing with us?"

"Is that really why you came here? To ask me that again?" I realize this time that I hope it is. Just working and going home is getting really lonely.

"Yeah," he admits. "That's the only reason I came, really. The rest was just an excuse. I'm a pretty lousy liar."

He is.

Inside, I put in his veggie burger order. Placing a tall orange soda with no ice in front of him, I lean against the opposite table, since we're not allowed to sit with the customers. "How did you know I wanted orange with no ice?" he asks, clearly pleased.

"We used to rehearse together three times a week," I say. "And when we went out afterward you always ordered orange with no ice."

"I didn't know you were noticing," Niles replies. He's flirting.

"I noticed," I flirt back.

"Or is it that you have super memory now?"

"That, too," I say. "It's very strange. Everything I remember is very sharp, totally clear. Like, I used to remember going to the beach when I was little. I love the beach, and it's a good memory. Now, though, when I think of it, I can hear the crash of the waves and the screams of the gulls. I can feel the itch of the sand in my suit. It's so vivid that I have to scratch."

"That must be nice," he says, "except for the sandy bottom."

"It is, but it works with every kind of memory. Bad ones, too."

Immediately, I wish I hadn't said that.

"Like the accident?" Niles guesses.

I nod grimly while fighting back the impulse to resurrect that memory. It's too late. The tearing of metal roars in my ears, as does the sound of Matt and Niles shouting. And the pain! The searing burn of torn flesh, the fiery agony as my bones cracked.

I feel it all as though it's happening over again. With this new ability that's getting stronger all the time, I experience agony that I never recalled before. This time is stronger than the last. What will the next memory bring?

I don't want to go through this the next time.

Niles stands abruptly. "Whoa!" Bracing my arms, he lowers me into a chair. "Steady there, Supergirl. You're about to faint. Put your head down."

I do and the blood trickles back into my brain. It helps, but not totally. I keep seeing Matt's blood-smeared face. I smell the gasoline and hear the screaming. "Get back! It's going to explode." I feel the firm grip of the firefighter dragging me away.

These flashbacks and other horrible ones—the agonizing ride in the ambulance, the many surgeries, the days of nausea and slow recovery—have happened to me a lot in the last two weeks.

I've developed a trick for controlling it.

With a lot of concentration, I focus on a white screen in my mind. When thoughts try to enter the white, I turn them into a rubber ball and bounce them out again, as if my mind is a handball court. All I want is the blank wall.

Keeping my mind under that kind of control all the time is difficult. The alternatives are worse, though. Other people have buried—suppressed—memories. I want these to go even deeper underground.

Karen hurries by. "Your order is up, hon."

Then she doubles back, noticing the state I'm in.

"What happened?" she asks Niles.

"She almost fainted."

I lift my head, still crouched on the chair. "I'm okay."

"Stay there. I'll get you some water," Karen offers.

I pull myself straight. Though I'm a lot better, I still feel weak.

"Feeling any better?" Niles checks.

Nodding, I wipe my sweating forehead with a napkin. "Some memories are better forgotten," I say.

13

"You've changed so much!" Sylvia Marcus says when I enter her office at Snap Girl. I'm about to shoot my first Snap Girl commercial.

I smile, preparing for her to gush. So I'm surprised by the worry that clouds her face. I've never looked better in my life—so what's the problem?

"It's the new me!" I tell her, smiling wide.

"You look great, but for us the old you was better," she says.

"Are you kidding?" I cry. "I'm more in shape than ever. My hair keeps getting thicker, my skin is practically glowing, my muscles are more ripped."

"Exactly. You were a regular girl who needed lots of Snap Girl products to improve her look. Are you even wearing makeup right now?"

"No," I admit.

Sylvia hunches, propping her chin on two fists as she scrutinizes me. "I'm a genius," she says after a moment. "We'll do a before-and-after sequence with you. We'll use the Polaroids we took of the old you and then juxtapose them with photos of the current you."

"And you'll say it's because I use Snap Girl makeup?"

"We'll put some on you, of course."

"I'm not wearing it right now, but I have been wearing it."

Sylvia stands, then comes around to the front of her desk. "That's wonderful! That was you then. This is you now. It's all essentially true." She studies me once again. "Why *do* you look so fabulous, if I may ask?"

"I have a chip in my brain that helps send messages to my fake arm and leg. It also helps with the brain damage that I—"

"The important thing is that it's working," Sylvia says, cutting me off. "Let's get you to makeup."

At the door, she stops. "I wonder . . . do you think I could get a chip like that?"

"I don't know. I mean, I was in a nearly fatal accident with an oil truck."

"Hmm. Right. But still . . . there's got to be a way."

"It would probably be extremely expensive," I say as we head down the hall together.

"Yeah, well, so is a facelift, and it doesn't have all the other side benefits. I would kill for your hair alone."

That Sylvia is so enthused is a relief. For a moment I thought she wouldn't use me for the commercial. The money will be great.

Diner customers constantly recognize me from the news pieces, which is a thrill for them and for me. I'd like to keep it all going, especially the money.

Just as we're about to head into makeup, a man in a suit pulls Sylvia aside. They speak in agitated tones and glance my way constantly.

Sylvia returns to me looking apologetic. "Did you quit school, Mira?"

"It just didn't, uh, seem relevant anymore," I say. "I'm just so beyond that now. Old me, new me. You know. And I'll need to be available, since I'm working for you now."

"Which means you're no longer a high school swimming champ, am I right about that?"

"Right."

"You're a diner waitress now?"

"How do you know all this?"

"We have people who research. We like to be current with our spokespeople. I'm sorry to tell you this, because you do look fabulous, but my boss just told me we can't use you. High school dropout diner waitress who uses Snap Girl cosmetics is not the image we're after."

"Everyone doesn't know that," I argue. "I could go back to school, even quit the diner."

But I'm already gone in Sylvia's mind. I can see it on her face.

She holds out her hand to shake. "You're so inspiring. I hope it all works out well for you. Good luck, Mira"

Feeling strangely numb, I take the elevator down. As I step off, the lobby spins. I reach for something to grab on to but claw at air . . .

. . .

My eyes open and Dr. Hector looks down at me. "Had a nice nap?"

The room looks just like the last hospital room I was in. "What happened?"

"You're okay now."

"What happened?" I repeat.

"Your blood pressure went a little crazy. We've got it under control, though. Has this happened before?"

"Once. Twice maybe." I don't know that blood pressure caused the fainting, but it probably did. "Can I go home?"

"Not yet. Your mother just left, but we talked about something we could try, in order to avoid this happening again." He goes on to explain that he wants to essentially implant a more powerful chip that should make every system in my body work at even fuller efficiency. "Right now the signals from your brain aren't being fully communicated and it's causing your nervous system to work overtime. The stronger chip should take the burden off your nerves, and therefore lower your blood pressure."

"I can't keep fainting like this," I say. "I don't want that."

"Of course not."

So, I have yet another operation.

• • •

The sun pours into the room, making everything sharper, more detailed, like it's been through some kind of high-definition film process. Sitting up in bed, I breathe deeply. Is oxygen being pumped into the room? It must be because each inhalation makes me more energized.

To be honest—I feel absolutely great.

• • •

I don't know why they're keeping me. They've been telling me I'm here for observation, and my mom won't do anything when I complain to her. "Listen to the doctors, honey, they know what they're doing, and we all want what's best for you."

But after a day I wonder what's stopping me from leaving. My bag and clothing are in the closet. My artificial limbs sit nearby.

I can take the train from here. It's only a few miles to the train station, not a bad walk. What's to stop me? I'm sick of being caged in this room.

In a few minutes I'm down the fire stairs and out the door, texting Mom. **I'll be home in a while. No worries.**

• • •

The guys from Electric Storm are blown away when I walk into their rehearsal. "I'm ba-ack," I say jokingly.

"Mira!" Niles says. "I saw your mom. She told me you were in the hospital."

"I was—and now I'm out."

"She said you fainted again," he says.

"They fixed me, so I'm better than ever." I smile at them all. "Still need a singer?"

They look to one another, probably recalling the mess I made of "Urban Creep" the last time I tried.

"I was still recovering last time," I say. "I'm in way better shape now. I wouldn't force myself back into the band if it turns out I'm still terrible."

"Are you sure?" Matt asks.

"Go ahead," Niles says. (Still with the cane. What is going on with him?) His eyes shine reassuringly.

I don't need encouragement, though. I can do this.

They start playing and I step to the microphone. "Urban cree-e-e-p," I croon. I'm stunned. This isn't even my voice. "From down deep, I see you even in my slee-e-e-p . . ."

My throat reverberates, vocal chords twanging like guitar strings. The notes surge from my diaphragm, bursting into air. "Dreams of you on the street, running steps, the night's own beat!"

I'm killing! I don't need to see their faces to know it's amazing.

The song ends and no one says a thing for a long moment. Finally, Tom breaks the silence. "Mira, what happened?" he asks. "Did you swallow an amplifier?"

"Have you been taking voice lessons?" Matt inquires more seriously.

"They implanted me with a new, more powerful chip," I tell them.

"When?" Niles asks.

"Yesterday."

"Yesterday?! Mira! You had brain surgery a day ago and you're here today?" Niles cries. When he puts it like that it does sound nuts.

I shrug. "I feel good." The guitar he holds gives me a new idea. An image, a memory of him playing it comes to me. "Can I use your guitar a minute, Niles?"

Niles looks puzzled, but he hands it to me.

"Mind if I play it?" I ask.

"Can you?" he asks, nodding toward my bionic arm.

I'm not sure. Up to now I've just been playing rhythm on my own acoustic-electric guitar. But I have a sharp image of watching him. My prosthetic fingers buzz electrically, my excitement zapping signals to them. I recall not only Niles but every video I've ever seen of a lead guitarist.

With my right hand on the frets, I run my bionic fingers up and down the neck of the guitar like lightning.

When I'm done, the guys are wide-eyed.

"Sings like Adele and plays like Slash," Tom says quietly.

"Better than Slash," Matt murmurs.

"All through the miracles of science," Tom adds.

I grin, so pleased with myself.

Niles says nothing, though. He sits off to the side, pale and a little blank. "Are you okay, Niles?" I ask.

He startles as though I've called him back from some distant place in his head. "Yeah, yeah . . . no . . . I'm fine. That was awesome, Mira. Amazing!"

"I was remembering the way you play," I tell him.

He grins. "I wish I was ever that good."

My phone rings in my front pocket. I know from the ringtone it's Mom. It's my imagination, but somehow the ring sounds angry.

"Are you going to pick up?" Niles asks.

I cringe. "She's going to be mad at me."

"Yeah, well . . ." Niles gives me a face that says, *No kidding.* The phone is quiet for a moment and then starts again. "She's got to be super worried," he adds.

"I left her a message," I say.

"Come on, Mira." He's right. Digging the phone from my pocket, I answer. *Mad* is putting it mildly. She's so upset that I can't get a word in. She's coming right over! Mom gets off the call without even saying good-bye.

The guys stare at me and I stare back, not knowing what to say. I begin gathering my things and stuffing them into my backpack. "It was a bold move," Matt says.

His attempt to be supportive makes me smile. "Thanks, but it probably wasn't the brightest idea I ever had."

"No, I guess not," Matt agrees. "Still, it was gutsy. It goes with your whole Supergirl thing."

"You're feeling good, right?" Niles asks.

"Yeah," I reply truthfully, "more than good . . . I feel better than I have in my whole life."

"Really?" he questions, looking doubtful.

I nod. Then a squeal of brakes sounds from the driveway and my heart races. I can't believe how quickly Mom got here.

"Bye, guys," I say.

"You sounded awesome," Tom says with a weak wave.

Niles throws me a smile. It makes me feel that whatever happens next won't be so bad.

When I get into the car Mom's jaw is clenched and she

doesn't even look at me. "Mom, I just couldn't stand it there any—"

"Don't speak," she commands stiffly. "There's no excuse you can possibly have." She reverses out of the driveway, and from her direction I know where we're headed—back to the hospital.

14

More boring days of rest and physical therapy. Brain scans, blood tests, so many electrodes on and off. I hear the monitors constantly beeping even in my sleep.

Here's the thing, though: I'm getting stronger—a lot stronger. I imagine a current of white light streaming from the copper chip in my brain, spreading into the tips of my fingers and toes. This light is a rod of energy that's so powerful it can't be broken, not even bent. It's just a feeling, but it never leaves me and every day it's more intense.

Then after about a week, I hear from a nurse that I'm to be released. Dr. Hector comes into my room but he's not smiling. "How are you feeling, kiddo?"

"Great!"

He scowls though I expected him to smile. "On a scale of one to ten?"

"Ten! Eleven!"

"Dreaming?"

"Every night."

"Nightmares?"

"The opposite," I tell him. "Last night I dreamt I was flying."

"Ever dreamt that before?"

"Sometimes, but this dream was different. I was in outer space. I circled the space station."

"Okay," he says. "Listen, we're sending you home today. All your tests show that you're in great shape. Amazing shape. But you have to promise to stay in touch. If anything out of the ordinary happens, let me know right away. We're sending you an online check-in app. I want you to fill it in every week and send it to me. Can you do that?"

"No problem."

"Excellent. Don't forget." He extends his hand and we shake. "Pack up. When you're mom gets here you're a free young woman."

· · ·

I'm only home an hour when the doorbell rings. I know it's Emma, since she'd texted to say she's coming. "Look at you!" she cries, coming into the kitchen where I stand at the stove making my usual can of tomato soup. "You're like a supermodel! What happened?"

"I'm super bionic girl," I joke with a laugh.

She slides into a kitchen chair. "This is seriously weird," she says. "Though I like the partially shaven head look. It's very rock star."

I tell her how I fainted and Dr. Hector did the chip upgrade, careful to skip over leaving the hospital early. Given how much trouble I got into with my mom, I don't want Emma freaking out on me, too.

"I want a chip," she says. "And I'm only half kidding."

My phone buzzes with a call from Niles. "Can you go with us to Poughkeepsie this Thursday?"

"Sure," I say. "I'm not working this Thursday. What's in Poughkeepsie?"

"That club, The Second Chance. Matt persuaded the guy there to audition us. This could be huge for us, create a real following."

He tells me we're going to rehearse for the next two days. I'm excited, but then I think of something and my whole body tenses up. "Who's driving?" Once more, the awful memory begins to rise—the crashing, the screaming, the mind-bending pain.

"Mira?" Niles sounds so far away.

"Mira," Emma says right in my ear, her hand on my good shoulder anchoring me back down to Earth.

I'm stronger today than I was in the diner. I can push the memory back down. "It's okay," I tell Emma and Niles. "I'm okay. I'm over it."

There's silence on the other end. "Niles?"

"Maybe it's too soon for you to get into the van again. How about Matt drives the guys and I'll pick you up in my car?"

That sounds nicer, so I agree. I hang up just as the soup bubbles, and Emma reaches around me to turn the burner off.

"What's going on?" she prompts me eagerly. "What about Poughkeepsie?"

"The band has an audition for a club there—the first the guys will have played in months," I say. "I'm sorry I freaked out—it was the prospect of getting in the van after . . . well, so Niles and I are going to drive together instead and meet up there."

"You have a date with Niles!" Emma says.

"It's an audition, crazy," I correct her.

"I think you like Niles, though. Don't deny it."

"I might be taller than he is, now that I've grown."

"Who cares?!" Emma cries.

"You don't think we'd look silly?"

"No! He's adorable. He likes you, too."

I know he does. But how do I feel about him? Do I want to be more than friends?

• • •

"It went great, didn't it?" I say to Niles as I climb back into his old Civic after our audition. The manager of the place hardly believed what he was hearing. It was written all over his face. When he said he wasn't certain, that he had to think about it, I knew he just wanted to get our price down.

"The guy was blown away," Niles agrees. "I'm sure we got the gig."

I am, too.

Niles hasn't even started the car yet when Matt texts to say we're on for the following Friday. We jump into each other's arms—but then pull away awkwardly.

Not that far, though. Our eyes meet. There's an electric charge running between us that I've never experienced before. Not with Jason. Not with anyone.

Suddenly we're kissing. I don't know how it starts. We lean over the steering console, pressing our lips together.

We stop to gaze at each other, checking that we're both okay with this.

We're more than all right. I've never felt so all right in my life. "Is this real?" I ask. It feels real to me. It feels like the start of something completely new, and completely comforting and familiar, both at the same time.

"It's real," Niles replies. "It's real for me."

"Me, too," I say and somehow I know it's true.

• • •

I can't stop thinking about Niles, even if I want to. He plays on an endless loop in my head. The way he smelled of almond soap. The feel of his lips against mine. The sound of his voice. *It's real for me.*

With Jason, I never obsessed. Jason was there. It was nice to have someone special. We got along most of the time.

Niles has been there all along also. Until recently I never thought a lot about him. Then, suddenly, he's taking up all the room in my mind.

Is he thinking about me in the same way? He must be, because he texts a lot, more than he ever used to.

To take my mind off Niles so I can concentrate on playing, I get out my guitar. I'm curious to see if I can reproduce the sound I got the other day. Finding some YouTube videos on my phone, I study different guitarists closely, willing myself to memorize every move they make. I'm astounded at how easily I can visualize what these guitarists are doing with their hands.

Can I reproduce it on my own guitar? Not exactly. Plus, it's a mishmash of styles. But I like the way it sounds. It's my own and I'm happy with it.

I don't think of Niles while I'm involved with the guitar. I'm so engrossed that I barely make it to my shift at the diner on time. But once I have work to focus on—the orders to put in and coffees to fill and checks to tally up—my brain doesn't wander to music or Niles even once, and it's almost a struggle to pull my mind away as I walk to Matt's house for rehearsal. I wonder if the new chip can do this, give me powers of concentration and intense focus that I've never had before.

Matt's written a new song he wants us to try. The lyrics are about love, but I notice there's a lot of colliding, crashing, and smashing imagery. It reminds me I wasn't the only one in the van that day. The title is "Love Meltdown." It's not a bad song.

The arrangement calls for Niles and I to share a microphone and harmonize. We sound great together even though I have to be careful not to drown him out with my newly powerful voice. When our faces are close, he smiles at me with his eyes. I love that there's a secret between us!

Matt's written in a drum solo for himself. It gives Niles and me a chance to dance together. It's not the same as before. The cane slows Niles down. He shuffles and sways.

Matt stops playing when his solo is done and calls for a break. "Niles, maybe you should let Mira dance alone," he suggests as we all move into his kitchen. "That cane is messing you up."

Niles turns to me. "Sorry," he says.

"I didn't notice anything wrong." A white lie.

"Mira, do you think you could play like you did the other day?" Matt asks, twisting open a bottle of water. "Could you do it again?"

This time I've brought my guitar. "I've been practicing," I tell them. "I'm pretty sure I could do it again."

Matt and Tom move off into the den beside the kitchen,

leaving Niles and me in the kitchen. Do the guys know something's going on between us? "Did you tell the others about what . . . happened the other day?" I ask.

"What happened?" he asks, his face a blank. Can he be for real? Is he teasing?

I must look completely disappointed that he doesn't think our kissing was the major event that I think it is. Then my face clouds over defensively. "I mean, it's not like it was a big deal if you don't want it to—"

Niles takes my wrist and draws me closer. "Kidding! Sorry! I was just kidding. Of course it's a big deal. It's a huge deal. It was a stupid thing to joke about. Sorry." He scowls. "Wait. You don't think it's a big deal?"

"I just said that because I . . ." What an idiot I am!

"Because why?" he prompts gently.

To hide my embarrassment, I let my forehead drop to his shoulder. "I just meant that if you're not that into it, it's okay."

"I'm into it, into you," he says and then laughs lightly. "SO into you."

The signal my bionic limbs receive from my brain is ecstatic. I'm thankful my leg isn't carrying me off in a happy dance all over the kitchen.

Then a less joyful thought slows down my exuberance. "Does it bother you that I'm . . ."

"What . . . beautiful, talented, fun to be with?" He holds me close with his hand on the small of my back.

I raise my bionic hand, nodding toward it. "No. This."

"No, it doesn't bother me that you've been through a major accident and have managed to survive it. I like that you're brave. And strong."

"Really strong," I say with a small laugh. "Like . . . robot strong. You'd better never make me mad." I curl my robotic fingers into a fist but I'm smiling.

Niles turns his head close to me. "I never want to make you mad at me," he says as he leans in, kissing me softly on the mouth. "Never." Kiss. "Ever."

· · ·

On the big night that we play at The Second Chance, we open for another group that has a regional following: Zombie Rant. The local radio station plays some of their songs occasionally. We walk onstage to the sound of groans from the audience. A guy shouts, "We came for Zombie Rant!"

I tie my hair to one side with a leather cord so that the shaved part of my head will be obvious. *Edgy*, as Dr. Hector says. In my dark skinny jeans and bleach-splotched T-shirt I feel good. My boots are beat up from years of wear and nobody can tell I'm balancing on half an artificial leg and foot. I make no attempt to conceal my prosthetic arm as I grip my guitar.

Emma and a friend of hers named Toni are in the audience. I peer out over the crowd, searching for her. She's in the front mezzanine and waves. Raising my bionic arm, I wave back.

The club darkens as the stage lights shine on us. We begin "Urban Creep" while the audience continues its restless chatter. We play, exchanging worried glances. We have to find a way to turn this around—but how?

"Next we'll do 'Love Meltdown,' okay?" Matt suggests.

We launch into it. Matt nails the drum solo, but when his drumming stops, the audience barely notices. I give my guitar work all I've got, shutting my eyes and sending nerve signals directly to my fingers. They fly! This has got to grab their attention.

It doesn't.

"Zombie Rant!" someone shouts.

We carry on to the end of our dismal set, trying our best not to give it up and walk off. I was so excited about my new abilities—my new voice, my guitar skills, the band's whole new sound and new songs. I never expected this.

We don't bother to stick around for Zombie Rant. Emma and Toni wait for us backstage. "You guys were great," Emma says.

"Really great," Toni agrees.

"Could you even hear us though all the noise?" I ask.

Emma and Toni look at each other, not knowing how to answer. "That wasn't your fault," Toni says.

"It's our fault that we couldn't keep their attention," I disagree. "I don't know what went wrong. I thought we were good."

"You were really good," Emma says.

"Next time we have to be better, or louder."

"Our amplifiers were turned all the way up," Tom says. "We couldn't have been louder."

"Then we need stronger amps." I want Electric Storm to be major, not an opening act. If we have to get better than we are . . . then that's what we have to do.

15

Niles and I don't talk much as we drive down Route 9 that night. We're too bummed.

"Tomorrow might be better," Niles says as he pulls into the gas station. We're booked for the entire weekend.

"It's already tomorrow," I say without any enthusiasm.

Where did we mess up? The band rocked. I thought my vocals killed, but apparently I was wrong. It's hard to hear yourself objectively. People singing in the shower think they're awesome, when in reality . . . not so much.

While Niles pumps gas, I head into the convenience store for snacks. As I enter two guys a little younger than me are near the counter. "Hey, Electric Storm Girl!" the taller of the two says.

It's surprising but nice to be recognized. "Hey," I reply with a wave and a weak smile.

"I told you it was her, Adam," the taller kid says to his friend. "I saw them on YouTube."

"They're on Twitter, too," Adam says. Then he turns to me. "You played at The Second Chance tonight, right?"

"How did you know that?" We're nearly ten miles away from there.

"I saw you and your band on Tumblr. It's all over Twitter and Facebook, too. Want to see?" he offers, extending his phone.

"Sure." Clicking the link brings me to a video of "Love Meltdown." The audio is playing from a phone so it's a bit tinny. Just the same, I'm smiling. We sound good.

Niles comes in so I show it to him. "Wow!" he says. "How come you can't hear the background noise—all the people talking?"

"Someone standing in the wings must have taken it," the taller kid says as I hand him back his phone. He scans it a moment before handing it back to me. "Catch this action," he says.

The same video is on Twitter but with a different person tweeting. Hashtag: ZMBIRANTFANSRJRKS.

Thanks, Emma, I think. But a second look and I see it's not from her. It's a complete stranger who follows The Second Chance. The phone buzzes and Emma's retweeted the video. And the mentions keep coming.

"You should respond—keep the buzz going," Adam says.

"What should we say?" I wonder aloud.

"Write that the band and their fans suck," Adam suggests.

"No," Niles objects. "We have to see them again tomorrow."

I dig my phone out and open the Twitter app. "We should take the high road," Niles says. "It's classier."

So Niles and I each tweet about how Zombie Rant fans were just excited to see their band and how there's room for everyone in music. Tom and Matt are more up for a fight in their tweets but they cool down quickly when they see what we're tweeting.

"Instagram is on fire with you guys," the shorter guy tells us as photo after photo of the band flash by.

"Do you have music for sale?" Adam asks.

Niles and I shake our heads.

"You should put some up online somewhere," the taller kid says. "Do it right away."

We thank the two kids. I treat them to the bag of chips and sodas they were about to buy and then pay for the Yoo-hoo, water, and pretzels we're buying.

Outside, Niles has pulled his car to the side. We climb inside and put Matt and Tom on speaker on Niles's phone. Together we figure out how to sell "Love Meltdown" for a dollar a download.

"That's not very much," I say.

"In ten hits we'll have ten dollars." When Niles puts it like that it suddenly seems possible we might make some money.

"Look on Facebook." Tom's voice comes from the phone resting in the console. "Your friend Emma's post has two hundred likes already."

Emma *Likes* the Electric Storm page, so they're all seeing her post. She's written: **TALENT OVER TALK** and posted the same video that the kids inside the convenience store showed us.

My phone buzzes with another notification. Someone has tweeted: **ELECTRIC STORM GIRL ROCKS OUR WORLD.**

I'm reading this as I sense that something is passing us at alarming speed. Before I can even look away from my phone, I hear the crash.

Niles and I leap from the car, leaving Matt and Tom shouting at us to tell them what just happened.

A driver has raced through the gas station and smashed into an idling car at one of the pumps. The car is now at a slant, with its trunk end up against a pump and its hood smashed into one of the pillars that support the roof covering the pumping area.

A woman screams. Turning, I see her, stunned and ashen, having just run from inside the store. Then I hear more screaming—screeching, really—from inside the car.

"Do you hear that?" I ask Niles.

"Hear what?" he asks.

The window is fogged but luckily my improved eyesight enables me to see clearly past the blur. A small boy is upside down strapped into his car seat. Instantly, I am all instinct, no thought.

Wrapping my bionic arm around the pillar, it's easy to pull up onto the car and scramble to the back window. The back door won't open. Locked. Hanging upside down, I attempt to crack the glass with my elbow, but it's no good.

People shout suggestions and warnings at me but I can't listen. I pull off the boot on my fake leg and use my titanium foot to kick the front windshield with all my strength—all of it, everything I can summon. I kick again, and once more. With a satisfying crackle, the safety glass forms a pattern of breaks along the windshield. More pressure and the glass gives way.

I chop at it with my heel until I'm able to slide through the opening and crawl to the red-faced boy. Fortunately, his seat unbuckles easily. He clings to my neck in a panicked embrace. Niles has climbed up onto the car, and reaches out his arms toward us. As I lift the boy through the car to Niles, I worry he'll be scratched by the sharp edges of broken safety glass, but there's nothing I can do about it. The important thing is to get him out.

Niles grabs the boy and passes him down to his mother.

As I climb out, sirens wail nearby. The woman sobs.

Niles grabs my left hand and pulls me away from the scene. "We should get out of here. This could all blow," he says.

We hurry to his car but don't get in because firefighters screech into the station, blocking our way out. They clear everyone away from the pumps before unleashing a torrent of water all over the area.

The local news van pulls into the far end of the station. Reporters and camerapeople head straight for me. "We've seen the videos," says Kate Osmer, a reporter I recognize from TV. "Less than a year ago Mira Rains was involved in a near fatal car accident also. Mira, how did you find it in yourself to take action now? It must have brought back horrendous memories."

She sticks the microphone in my face. I'm too stunned to speak. Horrendous memories? Oddly enough, no. After months replaying the accident in my mind, I'm suddenly blank.

"Will you be terrified to go to gas stations now? Your original accident occurred at a filling station, and now this."

"It's just a coincidence," I answer calmly.

"How were you feeling when you saved that child?" Kate Osmer pushes me to speak.

"Um . . . I wasn't feeling anything . . . I was just moving."

A man with a shoulder-mounted camera steps in front of us, and Kate Osmer faces him. "You heard it here," she says. "Without a thought for her own safety, Mira Rains—the bionic girl turned swimming champion—leaped into harm's way to selflessly save a small child."

The cameraman swings the camera to Niles and me. The blinding light at the top of his camera makes me blink stupidly.

• • •

When I finally get home, Mom is wrapped in her blue chenille robe and sitting in the living room. She claps her hand over her mouth and starts to cry. Hard.

"What's the matter?!" I hurry to her side, kneeling.

She can't answer me because she's sobbing.

"Mom, I'm fine."

She places her hand on my cheek as she continues crying. "I saw it on the diner's TV. It brought everything back."

"It's okay. I'm okay."

Why is she being so emotional? She can see that I'm fine. I texted that I was on my way home.

Zack comes into the room, rubbing sleep from his eyes. He goes to Mom's side to hold her hand. Lifting her head, she smiles up at him through her tears. His presence calms her. "I'm sorry," she says, wiping her eyes.

"It's okay," I say.

"You're a hero," Zack says.

"That car could have blown up," Mom wails.

"I think she needs tea," Zack tells me. Mom drinks chamomile tea when she's upset.

With a nod, I go to the kitchen to boil water. When I return, Mom and Zack are watching a video someone took at the gas station. It's on a regular TV station, not cable. It shows me passing the boy out of the car to Niles.

It's not fair that I'm getting all the attention. It took a lot of nerve for him to climb onto that car.

"I almost forgot," Mom says. "How did your performance go?"

"I'm not sure yet," I say.

She studies me quizzically but doesn't pursue it. "You must be exhausted," she says.

Now that I think about it, I'm not. "No," I say. Instead, I'm charged with energy. Probably it's all the excitement.

On the TV they show a clip of me saying, "I was just moving."

"You're not a hero," Zack says to me, his attention on the TV screen.

"No?" I ask with a smile.

"No." He studies me as though attempting to work out some perplexing puzzle. "You're a superhero now."

• • •

It's four in the morning. Sitting at the edge of my bed, I take off my left leg and my right arm. With my hand balancing me against my dresser, I stand to gaze at my image in the full-length mirror. I've taken off my makeup and my hair is up in a hair tie.

Some superhero.

My phone buzzes with a text from Niles. **You OK?**

Physically I feel fine. Nothing hurts. But isn't that a little strange? I should have some ache or strain—a bruise, at least. As I climbed out the windshield some sharp glass cut my arm. I'm sure of it. There's even blood on my sleeve. Now, though, there's not even a mark on my arm. Could I have healed that fast?

Yeah, I'm fine. You? I reply.

A little shaken, and wondering why you're not. Can you believe we were that close to another accident at a gas station?

Don't I seem OK? I text Niles.

IDK. Too calm maybe. Get some sleep—good night.

Am I in shock? I don't think I am.

But now I wonder if Niles is right. I should be relieved to have helped that boy. And I should be freaked out to have been so close to an accident after nearly dying in one less than a year ago. Yet I'm detached. It's as though everything has happened to someone else.

16

In my dreams I fly in and around buildings in Manhattan. It's thrilling and fun, so I'm grumpy about being awakened at eight o'clock by the buzz of my phone.

Leanna Humphrey? What does *she* want?

"Hello, stranger," she says in a super-friendly way. "I won't ask what you've been up to because it's all over the news."

"It is?"

"What? Do you live in a cave, Batgirl?"

"It's kind of early."

"I forgot. Rock stars stay up all night. You'd better go online."

"I will," I say, still groggy.

"Go ahead. And, in the meantime, let's make a date to hang out. We have to catch up."

"Yeah. Sure." I don't know why I agree to it. "I'll call you."

"Don't forget."

"I won't."

I feel as fake as my bionic limbs, and not nearly as energized. I've been just as phony as Leanna. But why? I admire people who don't play stupid mind games. I resolve to be more honest with people, even those I don't particularly like.

The next to call is Emma. I have to click with my left hand because I haven't even strapped my arm on yet. "Madame Suza sent an email," she tells me. "She says it's important that we see her as soon as possible."

"What?" This is weird.

"She's had a psychic flash about you."

Oh, man! First Leanna, now Madame Suza! It seems everyone is interested in me since I'm on TV. "Couldn't she tell you about her flash over the phone?"

"I guess not."

"My shift at the diner starts at three today. I can go with you tomorrow morning."

"Not before work today?"

I'm not sure I'm up to seeing Madame Suza today. "Let me have breakfast and I'll call you back," I say.

"All right. I'm proud of you, by the way. What you did was really brave."

"Thanks. It didn't feel like I was being brave, though. I didn't decide to help or anything."

"But you did. That's what's important. Anyway, talk later!"

"Bye."

Missed call from Sylvia Snap Girl, my phone says. That's how

I have her listed in my contacts. Her voice mail says she's not there, so I leave her a message saying I'm calling her back.

Slipping my phone into the pocket of my white cotton robe, I head downstairs. When I reach the kitchen, Zack has finished breakfast.

"How did you sleep?" Mom asks me as she sips from her cup of coffee.

"Great!" I reply, peeling a slice of salami from the deli paper and folding it into my mouth. In the living room, I turn on the TV and surf the channels.

Leanna wasn't kidding.

I am everywhere!

Some morning shows rerun my old interview with the network news. A clip of Electric Storm at The Second Chance gets played all over the place. One newscaster even tells viewers how to buy "Love Meltdown" online.

My phone buzzes with texts and notifications that I'm being mentioned in tweets and Facebook posts. I can't keep up with it all but I do look at Matt's text: **3000 copies of Love Meltdown sold already!!!!!**

That can't be right. I text back: **300 or 3000?**

3 triple 0! And it's only 8:30 a.m.!!!

Karen from the diner calls to tell me that Dimitri, the owner, wants me to *not* come in to work.

"Am I fired?" I ask, though I can't imagine why I would be.

"I don't know," she answers, "but the place is already filled with people waiting for you to come in."

"That's good, though, isn't it?"

"The crowd is good, I guess. But Dimitri thinks it'll be chaos once you get here and people will stop ordering and just jam up the place."

For a moment after I hang up, I feel disoriented. Working at the diner gave me somewhere to be every day. I used to be a girl who went to school. I used to play lacrosse on the school team. Later I swam on the team. I had a boyfriend named Jason.

All those things have been swept away, and the diner was what I had to hold on to.

How do I define myself now?

I'm a cyborg.

I have to face the fact. I know that, technically, many people are somewhat cybernetic—hearing aids, implanted teeth, glasses and contact lenses, heart stents, plastic surgery of all kinds, metal rods and pins in bones, and performance-enhancing drugs.

But I've crossed the line from restorative cybernetics to enhanced cybernetics. I've had more than my lost parts and abilities restored. I'm *better* than before, enhanced.

The kitchen landline rings and Mom picks up. At first she's pleasant but gradually her tone turns fretful. "I don't know . . . I have to think about it . . . Will it really help her? She's been through so much already."

Mom's face is a mask of worry as I enter the kitchen. "Dr. Hector wants to give you a more natural-looking arm and leg. He says they will be lighter and easier for you to manage."

"So, let's do it," I say. This arm is very robotic looking, and I'd missed the older one, the one that looked more like a real arm. I wouldn't mind a nicer one.

"Tell Dr. Hector I want it," I say.

"There's more," Mom says. "They want to give you a leg that's more like the arm you have now, only it won't look robotic. It'll look more like the new arm."

"Count me in," I say.

"Are you sure?" Mom asks, "Can you really cope with another surgery? He wants to see us at the hospital tomorrow."

"Sure," I tell her. "But it has to wait. We have to perform at Second Chance tonight and tomorrow."

"Mira, this is important," Mom says.

"So is Electric Storm," I tell her.

17

Niles feels crummy. He's not playing with us tonight, Matt replies when I text him.

You talked to him?

His mom texted me.

His mom? What's wrong with him?

Didn't ask.

Guys! How could he not ask?

He won't answer me, I text.

He won't answer anybody.

What's going on with him?

IDK. We'll pick you up around 5:00 tho, k?

I do not want to get into that van again, but what choice do I have?

I sit in the back, I text.

Can you play Niles's parts?

I can try.

The next call I make is to Elana. She's Niles's neighbor so maybe she'll know what's going on with him. When she picks up she's very excited to hear from me. Can I get her tickets for the show tonight? I promise to leave comps at the door for her. "Have you seen Niles around?" I ask, trying to keep my tone casual.

"Now that you mention it . . . no. Haven't you seen him?"

"He's not picking up his phone."

"Did he get hurt when you guys saved that little boy?"

That never occurred to me. "Maybe," I say.

Punching in Niles's number, I wait for him to pick up. I can't believe he won't answer *me*. But he doesn't, so I leave a message: "I know you're there. Pick up! Come on! I'm worried about you."

For the rest of the day I get ready to go on. I disassemble myself and shower. There's no time to soak in the tub.

After I strap on my arm and leg again, I study my look in the mirror. What should I wear tonight? Why not really embrace the whole rock star thing—not that I own rock 'n' roll–type clothes. Searching my closet I pull out a pair of tight, ripped jeans and an old Rolling Stones T-shirt I found at a vintage store. A pair of scissors on my dresser gets a workout as I cut the shirt into a halter top. My old boots complete the outfit.

The look is good, but something's not right.

Feeling brave, I fish out a can of something called Volume Booster from my now-abandoned tote of Snap Girl products.

Once I've pumped it into my hair and added Snap Girl Super Spray, my hair is a mountainous mass of curls.

Heavy black eyeliner makes my eyes intense.

I'm ready to rock!

• • •

When we arrive at The Second Chance, kids are lined up around the block to get in, and the show isn't for another three hours. The manager is waiting for us at the back door and comes over to the van before we even get out. Matt rolls down the window.

"I hate to say this guys, but Zombie Rant won't play if Electric Storm is the opener," he tells us.

"What?!" I cry, leaning forward from the backseat. "Why not?"

"They didn't say, but I'll pay you half your price not to go on," the manager says.

"These people on line are here for us," Matt argues. "That's what's happening, isn't it?"

"Listen, kid, Zombie Rant has lawyers and they're going to sue me if you go on. I'll pay you for the night. Just go." He throws cash into the van and walks away.

No one talks as we sit in the van not knowing what to do next. In about five minutes, a guy and a girl around our age rap on the passenger-side window. Tom, who is seated there, opens it.

"We heard a rumor Electric Storm isn't playing," the guy says.

"That's right, man. They won't let us," Tom replies.

"But we paid to see you!" the girl protests.

"Get your money back," I say from the backseat. I'm mad that the club is doing this to us. It's not right.

I remember that we passed a park on the way in. "Guys," I say. "What if we perform in the park tonight?"

"Will they let us?" Tom asks.

"We'll be street performers," I counter.

"The guy paid us not to play," Matt reminds us.

"We'll give the money back," I say.

Getting out of the van, I tell the guy and girl to spread the word that there will be a concert in the park down the block. "Get your money back, if you can, and come on over."

I hurry around to the box office and cut the line, shoving the money into the window. The murmur is already spreading through the crowd that Zombie Rant won't let us play.

The van is waiting for me and I run to hop in. In less than five minutes we're scouting the area. Tom spots some boulders. "That would be perfect," he says, "if that middle boulder wasn't there."

"Stop the van," I say, "let me try something." I get out and scrunch between the two huge rocks. The rock budges as I put my shoulder into it. Soon I've made enough space for the others to slide in and help. My own strength amazes me. Even though the guys are helping, I know they couldn't do this without me. With the boulder pushed into a semicircle with the other large rocks, we've created a cool playing space. "We can plug into the van," Matt says. "I'll keep the motor running."

Before we're even finished unloading our equipment, kids start pouring into the park. It's already getting dark and lamp-posts are turning on. One is right next to the spot where we've set up. It's getting cold, though not unbearably.

By the time we begin the first number, we have about thirty people watching and more continue to walk in. Three police cars arrive. I worry they'll shut us down, but they only hang back, watching.

When I have to take the parts Niles usually plays, I worry. Closing my eyes, I envision his fingers moving along the strings. Concentrating, I attempt to merge my consciousness with the image, incorporate it into myself. All other thoughts are blocked. My only reality is guitar strings. All the videos I watched online of guitar players—they flow through me and into my fingertips.

The next time I open my eyes, a sea of people are on their feet, roaring cheers, pounding their hands in applause. The band stares at me, their expressions dumbstruck.

Slowly I realize: It's for me. I'm the one they're cheering for.

· · ·

We play in the park until ten and would have gone for hours more except the police insist we stop. Noise ordinances and the crowd has gotten too large. The feeling is so UP!

"Electric Storm is right!" one of the audience members, a guy with longish hair, says as we're loading our stuff in the van. "You guys really are electric."

"Especially her," Matt says, jerking his thumb toward me.

"You are a goddess of the guitar," the guy says, walking away backward. "A goddess!"

"What did you mean by *especially her*?" I ask.

"I mean, you're literally electric," Matt explains. "The electric guitar was streaming through all your circuitry tonight. You could almost see it. There was like a blue haze around you."

I've gotten so used to Niles jumping in to squelch the stupid things the guys say that I half expect him to be there. But, of course, he's not.

"She's become like Storm from the X-Men."

"She can't control the weather," Tom says over his shoulder as he loads the last of the drum set into the van.

"Storm can control weather *and* electromagnetic fields," Matt reminds him.

"I'm not a mutant," I say, unplugging the main cable from the van. A small spark crackles and I drop the cable. A light tingling runs through my body, and random images fly through my mind, as though a flip book is being ruffled. I fall backward onto the dirt. Tom and Matt pull me back up.

"I told you," Matt says.

It takes me a second to feel steady on my feet, and I panic, trying to decide what to tell the guys, until I realize they don't know what happened. They saw me stumble after being shocked, but no one knows that my brain fritzed but me. And I can keep quiet.

My phone buzzes with a text from Elana offering me a ride home. I tell the guys I'm going to take her offer. We'll pass Niles's house and I want to go by.

• • •

"Are you sure you want to do this?" Elana asks as she pulls up in front of the house down the road from her own.

"Don't wait for me," I say with a nod. "I already texted my mom that I'm staying at your place."

"Okay. Good luck." Elana pulls away and I stand in the driveway staring at the darkened house. I can't ring the doorbell. Obviously everyone is asleep.

I try calling Niles, but it goes right to voice mail.

I'm outside your house, I text.

No response. But Niles's Civic is in the driveway.

Most days I'd be hurt by his lack of answer, and would probably just go home and spend some time tossing and turning, wondering what I'd done, before falling asleep. But not now. Tonight I'm the rock 'n' roll electric guitar goddess, and I'm Storm, the controller of electromagnetic fields.

Determined, I go around the back of the house, looking up. A plaid curtain moves on the second floor. Niles steps into the moonlit window and then goes back. Found him!

A very convenient maple *almost* reaches his window. My bionic arm enables me to easily pull myself onto the lower branches. It's minutes until I'm near the window ledge.

Gripping the tree, I reach as far as I can to kick the glass. It's a stretch but I make it.

Right away, Niles comes to the window. He's so stunned to see me outside that his expression is comical. I gesture for him to open up, which he does immediately. "Mira! What are you doing?" His voice is a sharp, alarmed whisper.

With a wave, I gesture for him to stand back.

"Don't!" he cries as I spring from my branch, gripping the shutter beside the window. A creak makes me think it's breaking loose. It holds, though, and I'm able to slide into the window.

"You're insane!" he says, coming to my side as I lie sprawled on the floor.

I want to say, *I'm not insane, I'm super*, but that does sound crazy—although it's how I feel.

"Are you all right?" I ask, sitting. A small green light on my bionic arm flashes. I've never noticed it before. That's not good.

"I'm okay," he says, sounding uncertain.

"Why didn't you come to the show tonight? Why aren't you answering anyone?"

"I told Matt."

"Your *mother* did."

"I'm going to quit the band, Mira."

"What?! Why? This is out of nowhere. Why wouldn't you talk to us first?"

"Not really. I've been thinking about it for a while. I mean . . . you can play my parts better than I can at this point." He takes his phone from his pocket and shows me a video that someone in our audience tonight posted of me playing. I have to admit that I *am* pretty amazing.

"It's not me, it's the bionics," I tell him. I realize I'm doing that thing that girls aren't supposed to do, even though they do it all the time—I'm making my accomplishment seem less so the guy won't feel threatened by it. "I only played your part because you didn't show up. If you had been there, I wouldn't have had to."

"That's not the point," he says. "The point is that you did it way better than I've been playing and you should continue."

"After all the months you were asking me to come back and try again, not to give up—you're just going to leave?" I say. "I don't want to be in the band without you."

"Just forget about me," Niles replies.

"Forget about you? Niles, didn't we just start kissing and all? I'm not hallucinating that, am I? I thought there was something kind of real between us."

"There is . . . I mean, there was."

"Then what happened?"

"It's not going to work, that's all."

I'm definitely missing something here. What's bothering him? It has to be about the rescue last night and all the attention I've received about it. "Is this some wounded male ego thing?" I ask. "It's not about the guitar playing, because that happened after you cancelled tonight. Tell me the truth!" I demand.

"You're famous now. You don't need me. I'll only hold you back."

"I might not need you, but I want to be with you. You've been a good friend to me, more than a friend. I want us to be together. I think . . . no, I do. I love you, Niles."

"No, you don't." He looks away.

"You don't feel the same way?" I ask. Now I look away. I want to cover my ears because I don't want to hear the answer I sense is coming.

"Forget about me, Mira."

"But why?"

"It's not going to work," he repeats.

"You don't feel the same about me as I feel about you?" That has to be it.

"No, I don't."

"So you were just messing with me, seeing if you could get me to like you."

"I wouldn't put it that way."

That Niles Bean is one of those kind of guys, the kind who chases a girl until he gets her and then drops her—well, I can't believe it's true. Not Niles!

"You'd better go," he says. Niles gets off the floor and sits on the edge of his bed. "Let yourself out the front door. Please don't climb out the window."

My body goes cold with disappointment and anger. How dare he just dismiss me like this? *Let yourself out.*

It occurs to me that with one swat of my bionic arm I could send him flying. And I'm that angry, too.

I'm also sad, though. I don't have a real desire to hurt him. As I gaze at him, he suddenly seems fragile to me.

As I go to the door, he tells me how to disarm the house alarm. "You could at least walk me to the door," I say.

"I'd rather not," he says.

Out on the street, it's gotten colder. A few months ago I would have broken down into a pool of tears. Now the urge doesn't come—I don't even feel them pricking the backs of my eyes.

18

The following week I'm scheduled for the new surgeries Dr. Hector has suggested. At the hospital, when I put my phone into a box of valuables for safekeeping, I'm glad to be rid of it. I'd never thought I'd say that—my phone is my connection to the world—but the attention around the rescue at the gas station combined with the viral popularity of Electric Storm is too much. One event feeds the other. My phone never stops buzzing.

"Ready for the big day?" Dr. Hector asks on the day of my surgery.

"Ready, I guess."

"You've become quite the celeb," he remarks.

"I know. Crazy, isn't it?"

An orderly comes in to wheel me into the operating room. I tense up. This is it. Showtime. I never get used to this. I'm scared every time.

Dr. Hector gazes at me with a serious expression. "You're a strong young woman, Mira," he says. "Hang in there."

. . .

When I wake up after five hours of surgery, Dr. Tim is there. Groggily, I check my chest for a scar but find none. "Didn't they operate?" I ask.

"Check your hip," he says.

It's covered with a black-and-blue bruise. "Laparoscopic surgery," Dr. Tim explains. "We made a small incision there and implanted the electrodes that way. Nerve impulses that would formerly have gone to your arm now go to move shoulder and chest muscles that still exist."

My new arm and hand are amazingly lifelike, covered in plastic flesh that matches the rest of me. The hand is a flesh-colored latex glove that covers the electronics.

There's a brief doctor-knock at the door, and a bald head appears. "Tomorrow we'll give you a leg and foot to match that arm," says Dr. Hector as he walks into the room.

"Will it work as well as the one I have now?" I ask. I wonder if I'll be able to use a flipper foot with this new type of leg. "I mean, will the natural look of it make it less effective?"

"Not at all," Dr. Tim says. "Trust me, this is the latest and the greatest in prosthetic limbs. They have all the capabilities of the more robotic-looking limbs, and are still activated by the chip in your head."

While he and Dr. Tim consult, Raelene comes in. "Hey there, Mira," she says with a smile. "Look at that arm! People will have to look mighty close to see that it's bionic." She has me open and close my new hand, flex my elbow, roll my shoulder back and forward. I can do it all.

Raelene remains after the doctors leave. Picking up the remote, she clicks on the TV. "How are you doing with all this, Mira?" she asks.

"Fine." My reply was automatic, so I pause to reflect on a real answer. How *am* I doing? "Dealing with all what?" I ask her.

"All the media attention."

"I'm handling it." That much is true.

"Are you enjoying it?"

That's a tougher question. Who doesn't want to be famous? It can only bring good things, right? "It's kind of overwhelming," I admit.

"How are your friends reacting toward you?"

"My real friends are cool," I say thinking of Emma, Elana, and the remaining guys in Electric Storm. Was it this new fame that drove Niles away? Is he so frightened by it?

"Okay," she says a little doubtfully. "Just please know that I'm here should you ever need to reach out. You've been through so much, and people keep telling you how lucky you are, but that doesn't mean that things aren't going to be upsetting or overwhelming."

I nod, grateful that she seems to understand some of what's been in my head the past few days.

Raelene produces my phone from her pocket. "I thought you might like to have this for a few hours—catch up with the outside world."

Although I was glad for the break, I'm ready to have my phone back. I check my messages, calls, Instagram, SnapChat, and Twitter accounts. I scan my emails—there are a ton, a lot of them from people I don't know, and plenty from friends and even people whose names I just barely recognize. But I admit, I'm particularly searching for any contact from Niles. I know this isn't smart. I should accept that he doesn't want to be a part of my life. I just can't believe he hasn't changed his mind, that he isn't going to apologize or explain.

Matt tweets that he hopes I get out of the hospital soon. A bunch of people favorite and retweet it. There's even a hashtag: ComehomesoonMira. So many people, people I've never met, wish me well.

But there isn't one call, text, or message from Niles.

I call him and it goes straight to voice mail. *This is Niles. Not answering calls right now. No worries. Just need some space.*

Suddenly, I'm certain that I've humiliated Niles in public. I should have let him rescue the little boy. I wasn't thinking. My only concern was getting the child out of the car. Now I've embarrassed him all over the Internet and the TV news.

I feel horrible and need to talk to him, to explain that he shouldn't feel badly. It's not his fault that he's not built like me—that he's not bionic.

Am I saying that it's not his fault that he's not as fast, sharp-sighted, and strong as I am—that I'm braver because I have all these enhancements?

Why shouldn't I say it? After all, it's true. It doesn't make him less than me. Most people are not bionic, at least not as thoroughly as I am. Is it possible that if Niles and I talk we can straighten this out?

Nice idea, I tell myself. *But clearly, it's not happening.*

Wanting to forget about Niles, I strap my leg to my stump and decide to stroll around the hospital.

In a lot of the rooms, doors are open and people watch TV. Every few feet or so, I hear my named mentioned on some news channel.

It seems I'm *trending*.

A young man in an army uniform waves to me. "The group is meeting in the day room," he says, gently taking hold of my elbow to lead me forward.

"What group?" I ask.

"The usual group," he replies. He's made a mistake about

who I am, but before I can explain he pulls open the glass door to the day room. Inside are ten or more young men and women, not too much older than I am. Most of them are wearing a prosthetic of some sort, either an arm or a leg. A legless young man sits in a wheelchair. His arm is artificial.

The army man leaves my side to approach the center of the room. A pretty young woman with her hair in a ponytail looks up at me from a couch. Both her legs are prosthetics. "What branch are you?" she asks.

"What do you mean?" I ask.

"Army, Marines, Air Force?" she says. "We were all injured fighting in the Middle East."

"I'm not in the service. It was a car accident."

"Oh."

She reaches to shake my hand. "I'm Amy."

"Mira."

"This group is really for vets, but as you can see, you have something in common with the rest of us, Mira. You should stay. It helps to hear how everyone copes in his or her own way."

"What part of the military are you in?" I ask.

"Army. Car bomb in Afghanistan."

"Sorry," I say.

"Sorry about *your* accident." Her eyes light with recognition. "Aren't you the guitarist champion swimmer girl?" I nod. "I've read about you. You have all the bionic stuff—the cable yarn muscles and the superchip in your head."

"That's me," I reply.

"You're so lucky," she says. "I'd love to have all that stuff. We all would."

I suddenly feel guilty for not being more grateful for all the advantages this science gives me. I *have* been lucky. "It's a lot to get used to, though," I tell her. "Some days I'm not even sure who I am anymore. I'm so different from who I was."

Amy reaches for my left hand and squeezes. "I get that. It's a big change."

The man who walked me in addresses the group. He talks about feeling different because you look different with a prosthesis. He speaks of the many challenges of dealing with an artificial limb. He talks about the problems it can cause with intimate moments between a couple. Then he asks for questions.

"Aren't you the girl who saved that kid?" a young guy, a soldier with a shaved head, asks me. When I say I am, he calls me a hero.

"You guys are the heroes," I say.

When the meeting breaks up, I'm equal parts sad and relieved. It was nice to be part of a group again. I didn't realize how much I've missed it. But at the same time, I felt so caught in the spotlight, when it wasn't even something I'd chosen. Part of me wishes I could pull off my arm and give it to one of the soldiers—don't they deserve it more than I do?

Against my better instincts, I call Niles again. *This is Niles. Not answering calls right now. No worries. Just need some space.*

• • •

Mom invites Emma's family over for Thanksgiving. Mom is friendly with Mrs. Schwartz, who is a short, cheery woman. Mr. Schwartz is her opposite, tall and quiet. Emma is their only child, so it's only the six of us.

Before we eat, Mom wants us to go around the table and say what we're thankful for. Mr. Schwartz is thankful that he wasn't laid off in the last round of firings at his company. Mrs. Schwartz is glad Emma got a scholarship to the state university at Binghamton.

Emma is grateful she got in, since it was her first choice. "I've decided to go straight through to get my master's in social work," she reveals.

"But what about your art?" I ask. "You said that artists didn't necessarily need college, and you've signed on for six years?"

"I can do art on the side," Emma says. "You were the one who convinced me to go college, Mira. Don't you remember telling me to take art classes that day when we were looking through the illustrated version of *The Tempest*?"

"I do remember, now that you mention it." It seems so long ago.

"It's great that Emma's on her way to college and a career she wants," my mom says, a little pointedly.

"It is," I agree. "You're allowed to change your mind. Life is full of changes, as I well know."

Emma giggles. "I think the number fifty-six is hanging over your head again. Change, remember?"

We smile at each other, happy to be friends.

When it comes to Zack, he shakes his head. He's not good at sharing his feelings.

"Are you grateful for butterflies and beetles?" I prompt him.

He nods his head vigorously.

"That's lovely," Mrs. Schwartz says.

Mom's eyes mist before she even speaks. "I'm so grateful that Mira is . . . Mira is . . ."

"Me, too, Mom," I say when it's clear she's too choked with emotion to speak. "I'm grateful to be alive."

• • •

I write a song called "Why Can't I Cry Over You?" The lyrics are filled with heartbreak and betrayal. They also ask a real question that's been on my mind. Usually I can't even see strangers cry without misting up. Lately, though, I just don't feel any urge to cry.

Maybe I never cared about Niles as much as I thought I did? I don't believe that's it, though.

I was more upset when Jason and I broke up—and he and I were together more out of habit than anything else.

Could it be that I'm more angry at Niles than sad?

19

DECEMBER

Sylvia Marcus phones me from out of the blue to tell me that she's left Snap Girl to open her own talent agency. She wants to be my personal agent. She also hopes Electric Storm will come on board. "I wanted to keep you all along," she says. "My boss has such old-fashioned ideas, though. It's why I absolutely had to leave the company. When I saw you again on the news, and read so much social media on your band, I was reminded of how truly fabulous you are. I think we could really achieve something wonderful together."

I run it past Matt and Tom and they agree. Our parents sign some papers giving permission, and she's our agent. It turns out that she's a great agent. Before the week is out, she's booked Electric Storm at Terminal 5 in Manhattan. We're not just the openers, either. We headline! All the Internet buzz, combined with TV coverage shoots us into the number one spot.

We are *so* trending.

. . .

"I want you to try this," Matt says at our next rehearsal. He holds up a guitar. "It's my brother's. But he won't care. He never plays it anymore." He hands it to me, smiling. "I'm a genius. I know."

I'm confused. "Why are you a genius?"

"It's a left-handed guitar," he tells me.

"I still don't get it. I'm right-handed." Actually, this isn't absolutely true anymore. One of the recent developments is that I now do a lot of things with both hands.

"That's a great idea!" Tom says as though he suddenly understands what Matt has in mind.

"Tell me!" I say. "What's going on?"

"Normally you would hold the guitar and play the chords with your left hand, correct?" I nod. "But maybe if you played chords and riffs with your bionic right hand, you could be amazing. It would be as if a machine was playing the chords."

"I'm not a machine," I say quickly.

"Don't be mad," Matt says. "You know what I mean."

"It could be really great, Mira," Tom says. "Try it."

Strapping on the guitar, I play a few riffs. With my new hand, I feel the strings. It's strange to play this way. "I don't want to change the way I play when we're so close to the show."

"Let's do it for today and see how it goes," Matt insists.

With a reluctant sigh I agree. It's not too long before I'm used to playing chords with my right and strumming with my left. It's sort of exciting, in a way.

That night I sit in my room and continue to practice until Mom tells me to stop because it's late. "I'm sorry to stop you when you're playing so well," she says, standing in my bedroom door.

"Really?" I ask.

"Really," she says. "I thought you had the radio on."

The thing is, I believe her. And it fits somehow—my machine hand, a backward guitar, and me.

. . .

"You need a whole new wardrobe," Sylvia tells me a day before the show. We're sitting in the theater, on break from a rehearsal. "It wouldn't hurt if you did something courageous with your superstrength, too."

"Like what?" I ask.

"I don't know. Leave it to me. I'll come up with something."

A man I'd seen working in the lobby comes to sit next to us. Sylvia introduces him to me as Stuart who runs the box office. "Pleased to meet you," Stuart says, shaking my hand. "I'm a fan. Love the last song you released on YouTube. Very moving yet hummable."

"Thanks."

"What's up, Stuart?" Sylvia asks him.

"Here's what I came to tell you. We just sold the last ticket. We're officially sold out."

Sylvia gives two thumbs up as she beams. "Electric Storm is on its way, baby!" she sings out.

"Mira!" Tom calls me to the stage. "Quit fooling around down there. Let's get this done."

Before he barked at me, I was about to tell them we were sold out. Now, though, I'm annoyed at his scolding, impatient tone, so I take my time getting up and I stroll onto the stage. "It took you long enough," Matt comments when I join them.

"I'm here now, aren't I?" I snap, annoyed.

"Sorry to bug you, your cyborg majesty," Tom comes back at me.

"What did you call me?!"

"You heard me," he says aggressively. Of course I heard him. (I hear *everything*.)

"What's your problem?" I challenge.

He mumbles in a tone so low that even I can't hear it clearly, but I catch some unflattering stuff, plus *mutant* and *cyborg*. Swear words are mixed in.

"Hang on a minute," I say. "We're headlining this show because of me. I'm the one with the fame. It's the cyborg who got us here."

"It was me who got you to play the left-handed guitar," Matt says angrily. "You were never that great a guitarist before that. Your robot hand does all the playing for you. Without it you're nothing."

"Yeah, well, without my robot hand *you're* nothing."

"Maybe we should all bow down to you," Matt says. "Is that what you want?"

A voice fills the theater. It's the sound guy sitting at the back with his equipment. "I can hear everything you're saying back here. You should all bow down to *me*. Quit bickering and let's get this done. I want to go home."

It takes another hour, but finally we have all the sound levels right. The guys head out to the van. "Are you coming?" Tom asks.

"I guess so," I say sulkily. I'm in no mood for them at the moment.

Sylvia approaches me. "Can we talk a moment before you leave?"

"Sure," I say heading toward her.

"Hey, we want to get going," Matt says. "Are you coming or not?"

"Let them go," Sylvia tells. "I'll give you a lift home."

I tell them to go ahead without me.

Sylvia says she needs to go over some paperwork with me, so I follow her up the theater aisle to the box office, where she says she's left the contract. When we get there, though, smoke fills the lobby. It's billowing out from under the door of the box office.

"Stuart!" Sylvia cries pulling on the knob. "It won't open. It's stuck or locked."

With my bionic arm, I yank at the doorknob, only managing to pull out the knob. "Call the fire department," I tell Sylvia, as I race around to the entry vestibule at the front of the lobby. The entire box office is filled with smoke. Through it I can see a figure slumped over the desk. Stuart's stuck inside.

Racing back to the door, I use my bionic elbow to smash a hole in the door. Reaching through it, I can unlock the door. The next second, I have Stuart under his arms and am dragging him toward the outside sidewalk.

What's taking the fire department so long? Shouldn't I be hearing sirens by now? Where's Sylvia?

I'm about to dash back inside to get her when she emerges from the theater holding her telephone up, using it as a video camera. Stuart sits up, suddenly seeming just fine.

It's then I realize that I don't smell smoke.

Sylvia sees me sniffing and smiles. "Dry ice machine," she explains. "Stuart remembered that they had one in the prop department."

I should be furious. They fooled me.

"Don't put that on social media," I say to Sylvia.

"Why not?"

"It's not honest," I tell her. "There was no real fire."

"You didn't know that."

Stuart climbs up, wiping his outstretched palm in a semicircle. "Bionic Lead Singer Saves Theater from Destruction!" He imagines the headline.

"Saves Box Office Manager from Death," Sylvia adds.

"Good-looking box office manager," Stuart amends.

"Sorry, guys, it was a hoax and I don't want any part of it," I insist.

"Too late," Sylvia tells me. "The video is all over Twitter and Facebook."

"Can't you take it down?" I ask.

"I could, but why? There's no harm done," Sylvia says. "If there had been smoke in the box office, you would have saved Stuart. It's not actually dishonest."

"I suppose so," I relent. Just the same, I don't feel right about it. "Is this why you offered to drive me home?" I ask Sylvia.

She nods, a bit embarrassed. "It was part of the whole . . . setup. Would you mind taking a train? I'll give you cab fare from the station."

"I don't mind," I say, which is true. At the moment the idea of sitting on the train alone without having to speak to anyone sounds good.

"Don't feel bad, Mira," Stuart says as I get into my coat. "It's only a publicity stunt. All big stars do it."

They seem so casual about everything, and I decide it's not worth getting mad about. I feel used and stupid, but I'm not seething with anger or anything. The only emotion I'm aware of is an emptiness, a *lack* of emotion.

20

At Grand Central there's a train to my town pulling out in fifteen minutes, so I buy a ticket from the vending machine and race-walk across the high-domed, grand lobby toward the track.

A cluster of young women point in my direction. They quickly obstruct my path. "Are you Mira Rains?" Their voices are bright, filled with excitement.

I want to say, *"Calm down. It's only me."*

"How does it feel to be bionic?" someone shouts from the back of the crowd, which is growing larger by the moment.

"Strong!" I reply. That I'm *strong* is about the only thing I know for sure. I don't think anyone wants to hear that I'm confused, lonely, alienated from the life I used to have.

One of them wants me to sign her hand, which I do. "I don't mean to be rude, but I have to catch my train," I say. That's not actually true. I don't *have to* catch it.

"You saved that man today," one of them says. "You must be exhausted. Wait! Do cyborgs get tired?"

That word, *cyborg,* is really starting to bug me. Am I some kind of freak? Do they think I'm a robot—a nonhuman? "I get tired like anybody else," I tell her, trying to break from the circle and continue to my train. That I get tired isn't exactly true, either. Ever since the last operation I only need about two hours of sleep. "I'm going to miss my train. Sorry," I say, sprinting toward the track tunnel.

"Look at her go on that leg," one of them says as I make space between us.

"I read that the other knee is bionic, too," another says, her voice fading behind me.

From the front of the train, I see the engineer watching, wide-eyed at the sight of me speeding down the ramp. I slow to a fast jog and am not even breathless when I slip into the second car. It's full of commuters with bent heads, engrossed in their newspapers, laptops, books, and reading devices. No one notices me and I'm grateful for that.

I'm headed for an untaken seat when I stop short. There's another vacant spot on the aisle even closer. I don't know if I should take it, though.

The passenger sitting beside the empty place, staring out the window onto the busy train platform, is Niles.

Passengers need to pass me and I'm blocking them. There's a chance he won't turn, allowing me to hurry by, head down, unnoticed. But as soon as I step forward, he looks straight up at me.

My smile of recognition is more of a tight, nervous lip twitch.

With his eyes riveted on me, Niles lifts his backpack from the seat beside him, silently offering it. Honestly, I'm happy for the unspoken invitation. I've tried so hard not to think of Niles, but it's been hard. Seeing him there, I realize all over again how much I've missed him.

"I'm surprised to see you. Why were you in Manhattan?" he asks. He's casual, as though there's never been any trouble, no harsh words, between us. This throws me because I'm not like that. Actually, I'm the complete opposite. I'm ready to resume our argument right from where we left off. (And I know exactly where that is, since I've rehashed the conversation in my head a million times.) Clearly, that's not going to happen, though.

I tell him all about Electric Storm playing Terminal 5. "That's so cool!" he says. Then a sad expression overtakes him just for a flicker and vanishes.

"Why were you in the city?" I ask.

"I had a doctor's appointment. I'm seeing a specialist."

He no longer has his cane. It's been replaced by two bright blue plastic forearm crutches that he's leaned against the seat in front of him. His legs seem thinner than I remember; there's a withered look to the way they bend. For the first time I realize he's slumped into the corner of his seat. I gaze up at him, my expression full of questions.

"Becker's muscular dystrophy," he explains.

I've heard of muscular dystrophy, though I don't know what this variety of it is.

"I got diagnosed when I had medical tests after the car accident," he says. "They checked to see why my leg wasn't supporting me even though the bone had healed. Turns out my muscles have been slowly growing weaker because of the disease."

So that's why he's been breathless and sitting, when he used to stand. Even though I noticed it I've been so involved with my own stuff that I didn't pay much attention. "Why didn't you say something?"

"I didn't want to talk about it."

"Do the guys know?" I ask.

Niles shakes his head. "Don't tell them, okay? I don't want anybody feeling sorry for me."

There are so many questions I don't know how to ask. Can he recover? Will it get worse? Will it kill him?

"Need a ride home? I could drive you. My car's parked at the station," he offers.

"You can still drive?"

"So far," he says.

That means eventually he *won't* be able to drive, which answers my first two questions. "All right. Thanks."

We zoom along, silently watching the scenery pass; first, apartment buildings, then lower buildings. The Hudson River shimmers in gold ribbons under the pink clouds of the setting sun.

"How do you like that new arm?" he asks after we've passed about three stations.

"I love it. I have even better sensation than before. I can feel everything the same as I do with my left hand."

He takes hold of my bionic hand, squeezing lightly, affectionately. Shutting my eyes, I inhale. His warm skin caresses my palm.

"Is it all right that I'm holding your hand?" Niles asks. His voice is all tender concern.

My eyes still shut, I nod. It's *so* all right.

"Mira, I'm sorry," he says. "I've been a jerk."

"No, me," I say quietly, looking at him once more. "*I'm* sorry. You were getting sicker and sicker right in front of me. I wasn't even paying attention."

"I shouldn't have pushed you away like I did. I guess my pride was . . . I don't know. I don't want you to see me as weak, especially when you're getting stronger and stronger."

"So this is all some macho guy thing?" I ask.

"In a way, I suppose so," he replies. "I told myself I'd disappear, cut everybody off."

I can relate. When I first came out of the hospital after the accident, that was how I felt.

"Niles," I scold mildly. "Didn't you think your friends would miss you, that *I* would miss you?"

The train rumbles on, filled with passengers. Even though there are people all around, to me, we're in a bubble of our own, just the two of us. "Did you . . . miss me?" he asks.

"Don't you know the answer to that question?"

"Not really. Did you?" His expression is so vulnerable. I feel as though I'm gazing right into his heart.

"I missed you more than I can tell you," I say. As soon as I speak I know my words are true. He's my true companion, my real friend; the boy whose kisses thrill me; the one who holds my hand so tenderly.

"Me, too," Niles says. "I missed you."

Lifting his hand, I press my lips to his knuckles. He leans closer and we're kissing each other. I inhale his woodsy smell.

Two things happen inside me at once: I'm crazy happy. My Niles is back. We both made mistakes but we've gotten past them. Is it fate? Is it luck? Did some force from another dimension arrange for us to be on this train at the same moment and reunite? Whatever the reason, I'm so grateful.

But in the same instant, I feel completely split from those feelings. I don't *feel* the happiness—or the joy or the gratitude. I want to so badly, but this isn't emotion. It's intellect. I know I should be happy. But I can't feel it.

I don't like this business of not feeling one bit. It scares me deeply. Terrifies me.

Niles stops kissing me. He gazes into my eyes with a worried expression. "Are you all right, Mira?" he asks.

"I'm fine," I say. "I'm so happy." I kiss him lightly. "Really, really happy," I say.

How can I say I feel *nothing* right now? He wouldn't be able to understand that. No one could. I can't even understand that.

Is it possible that what people seem to think about me is coming true? Could I really be turning into a cyborg?

21

When Niles drops me off in front of my house, I realize that my head is pounding. I find an over-the-counter pain reliever in the medicine cabinet and wait for it to kick in. It doesn't. All the lights suddenly seem way too bright. I've never had a headache this intense.

Zack sits in the living room on the couch watching TV. "I'm going to take a nap," I call to him, knowing Mom has just left for work. At the top of the stairs, I'm seized with horrible nausea and I make it to the bathroom just in time to heave my guts into the toilet bowl. With my head still pounding, I get to my bedroom but don't turn on the light. Instead, I lay in the dark, feeling miserable until finally I sleep.

When I awaken, I check my phone to discover it's three hours later. But my headache is gone. I wash up and then head down to check on Zack. He's still in the same spot in the living room, still watching TV. "Want some grilled cheese?" I ask.

"I made myself a grilled cheese already," he replies.

I look at him, impressed. "Shouldn't you be doing homework?"

"This is homework," he replies. "It's for Dr. Gersey." Dr. Gersey is the therapist Zack sees. She specializes in working with children on the autism spectrum.

Bending, I pick up the mail that's been left on the coffee table. A lot of bills for Mom but nothing for me except a postcard from the veterans' group I visited that day in the hospital. I vaguely remember adding my name and address to a sign-up sheet that was circulating around the room. It's an invitation to a holiday party somewhere in the city. Everyone in that group seemed so nice. Maybe I'll go. I stick the card in my back pocket to think about later.

Taking a closer look at the TV, I realize that the screen Zack is looking at shows a man from the shoulders up. Below him are written various emotions: happy, sad, frightened, worried, and confused. "I have to press the box next to the emotion I think the man is feeling," Zack explains. "When I get it right, another person comes on." I know that Zack has difficulty reading the expressions on the faces of those around him. Dr. Gersey likes him to practice with workbooks she gives him. This program is new to me, though.

Zack decides that the man looks worried. He uses the cursor on the screen to check the worried box. The man smiles and gives a thumbs-up before sliding off the screen to be replaced by the face of a woman. Zack has to decide if she's angry, suspicious, concentrating, or disgusted.

I decide she's angry. Zack selects disgusted. He gets the smile and thumbs-up. "How are you supposed to know the difference between angry and disgusted?" I ask.

"Can't you tell?" Zack asks. "I thought normal people could tell."

"You're normal," I say defensively, "just different."

"Like you?" he says.

"No, not like me," I say automatically. I'm not on the autism spectrum.

"We're both different now," Zack insists.

"Let me try this one," I say, taking the controller from him. A man slides onto the screen. It seems to me that his expression is blank. I select the box that reads *confused* because it's the only one that seems possible. A honking noise indicates I'm wrong. Next I click on *fatigued*. Wrong again! My next two answers are also incorrect. It turns out he's supposed to be *pleased*. "That guy does not look one bit *pleased*!" I complain.

The next face that comes on looks *frightened* to me, but the correct answer is apparently *worried*. "Ha!" Zack laughs triumphantly. "I'm better at the game than you are."

Handing the controller back to him, I get off the couch. "This thing makes no sense," I grumble.

Emma's name comes up on my phone as it buzzes. I pick up the call.

"Hey, Emma!"

"My tickets for tomorrow just came in the mail," she says. "I was so worried they wouldn't arrive."

"I would have gotten them for you."

"I wasn't sure you'd gotten my text, and I figured better safe than sorry. But tell me about practice! I saw that video of the fire."

"It wasn't a big deal," I tell her. "Nothing really happened, but my agent posted it anyway. But the ride home from the city was weird—what do you know about Becker's muscular dystrophy?" I tell her everything about meeting Niles.

"Poor Niles," she says. "How are you going to deal with this?"

"What do you mean?"

"I've got Becker's muscular dystrophy up on my screen now," she says. I've never met anyone faster on the computer than Emma. "He's going to be in a wheelchair by his twenties."

The image of Niles in a wheelchair forms in my head. "It might be different for everyone," I suggest.

"Sorry, Mira, but I don't think so. Becker's moves slower than regular muscular dystrophy, but it does get worse and worse. It says so right here."

"Is it . . . fatal?" This isn't easy to ask but I have to know.

"Let me see." The line is silent while Emma searches for the answer. "He has time," she finally tells me. "Forties."

Forties is a very young age to die, I know. Right now, though, it seems a long way off.

"How would you feel about living your life with a guy in a wheelchair? Is that a life you would want?"

"We're not getting married, Emma," I say.

"Not yet," she replies, completely serious. I suppose it *is* a serious question. I don't want Niles and me to ever break up.

"We'll deal with it as it comes, I guess," I say.

"This is terrible news," Emma says. "It's good that Niles has you."

I realize I haven't eaten, so I say good night to Emma and head downstairs. I'm surprised to see Mom on the stairs, heading up.

"There weren't many customers, so I got off a little early," she explains. "Zack tells me you can't pass the emotional intelligence test program."

"It's stupid," I say, hurrying past her.

"Slow down!"

"I'm hungry!" I snap.

Mom changes direction and follows me into the kitchen. "Why do you think that test is stupid?" she asks.

"It doesn't prove anything," I say staring into the refrigerator. "One person might express an emotion one way and another person would express it differently."

"True, there's a range. But most people can tell the differences."

"So what are you saying?" I turn to face her. "Do you think I'm autistic now, too?"

"Of course not! But lately I've felt that you're not yourself. Something's going on with you and I'm worried."

"Stop being so worried all the time, will you? I'm fine." Even though I'm worried about myself, I don't want to talk about it. This accident and having to rebuild our lives has caused her enough stress.

"You're not yourself, Mira!" Mom insists, standing.

"I'm aware!" I'm in no mood for this conversation. "I've changed a little, in case you haven't noticed."

"You've changed a *lot*, lately!" she comes back at me, raising her voice. "The only person who matters to you is you!"

"That is so not fair!" I say. Grabbing an apple from the fruit bowl, I leave the kitchen and go back up to my room. I'm sick of her constant nagging. So what if I can't pass a dumb face test? Emotion is overrated, anyway. Emotion only gets in the way of what a person needs to do to get ahead.

22

Tonight at the theater we connect with the audience from the start. Our sound is a little thin without Niles. If he doesn't return we'll have to replace him. The audience doesn't seem to care or notice, though. Tom and Matt and I bring the energy like never before.

My new leg is so strong that I can actually leap in the air while I play. My bionic super hand races up and down the strings of my guitar in a blur of motion. I've never played as well before. The clang of my final chords reverberates throughout the theater.

The audience is on its feet, shouting with the thrill of being lifted by the music. I look out over the audience. They've brought the house lights up just enough so that I can see their faces. I pick out Niles. Emma is there with Mr. and Mrs. Schwartz. Mom and Zack sit in the first row. Cell phones are held high, recording everything.

We wave good-night and turn toward the stage wings.

"One more song! One more song!" the people chant over and over. "One more song!"

The thunderous approval from the crowd deafens me. We count to twenty out loud together as we'd planned, hoping for this reaction. We return to the stage to perform our encore, an expanded version of "Urban Creep" that continues for a full five minutes.

When we finish, the audience goes crazy. They stomp on the floor and whistle, clap, and shout. We actually want to play longer, but it's against some rule of the theater. As we leave the stage once more, the techs bring the house lights up completely, signaling that we won't return again.

In the stage wings, Matt and Tom leap with joy, high-fiving and fist-bumping. "You were awesome tonight, Mira!" Tom says.

"Thanks," I say. "You all rocked!" I should be beaming, ecstatic. But it's more like a dream, something that's happening around me, not *to* me.

"Hey! Show some excitement, Mira! Tonight you became a true-life rock star," Matt says.

I'm pleased that we did well. It's always good to be successful. I know that.

"Big smile for the camera!" The photographer's flash blinds me. "Can you look happier, Mira?" he says. "They loved you out there!" I force a smile.

Niles stands in a corner by the curtain. I left word with the stage manager to let him back, along with Mom, Zack, Emma, and her parents. It's strange to see him so bent on his crutches. Matt notices him standing there. "Niles!" he shouts, waving him over. I've told the guys about his condition so they're not shocked. They punch him lightly on the back and tell him to return to the band.

He turns to me and our eyes meet. "That would be a great idea," I say. Only I hear my own voice as though I'm in a tunnel. My words echo in my head and I'm nauseated to the pit of my stomach.

Mom and Zack stand side by side, gazing around like lost lambs. I hug them. "You were great!" Zack says. He wears the wide smile I should have.

"Really terrific, honey," Mom says close to my ear.

I thank her, then tell her not to wait for me because I have to help pack up the van.

"Anything the matter?" Mom asks. "Something's wrong."

"No, nothing," I tell her. "Tired, maybe."

Worry clouds her face but she nods. "All right. Don't stay out too late. Tell Matt to drive slowly, it's supposed to rain."

Next I see Emma, who is elated at how great the show went. As soon as she hugs me she can tell I'm not into it. "What happened?" she asks.

"Nothing. This is all wonderful. It doesn't seem real, though."

"You're in shock," she decides. "You'll snap out of it. Give it some time." I don't want to tell her that this has been going on for a while. She'll only worry.

I return to the stage where the guys are unplugging equipment. Stagehands who work for the theater are doing the heavy lifting and moving. Niles sits on a stool, coiling a thick wire. He smiles when he sees me approach. "You okay?" he asks.

"I'm fine," I reply. "Just going to change before we leave."

"Okay." I'm heading for the dressing room, where my regular clothes are stashed, when Niles calls out to me. "You were really awesome tonight, Mira. It was amazing to watch you."

"Thanks." In the dressing room I pull on my jeans and realize there's something in my back pocket. It's the postcard I got from the veterans' group. I'd forgotten about it until now. JOIN US AT OUR HOLIDAY PARTY. It's being held at a place on the lower level of Grand Central Terminal, in one of the restaurants there.

I throw the card away and continue getting dressed. In the mirror I see I'm still wearing the heavy makeup I needed so I wouldn't appear washed out by the bright stage spotlights. In this lower lighting, I'm freakishly overdone.

The reflection of my face is so harsh it frightens me. Then I realize it's not all makeup. Blood is running out of my nose and I've smeared it across my cheek. With my head down, I hurry for the bathroom to get toilet paper to stem the bleeding.

In the bathroom, I wad toilet paper, holding it to my nose, smearing my makeup even more.

What have I become? Mira, the hard-hearted cyborg clown?! Smeared blood covers my face and hands. My eyeliner and mascara have turned into a sort of raccoon's mask around my eyes. How can I go back out there looking like this? I can't!

Getting away from the theater becomes my only thought. It's suddenly as necessary as breathing. I have to get out of here. There's not enough air in the room. If I don't get out, I'll die.

Grabbing my backpack from the dressing room, I bolt for the backstage loading dock door. It's raining, but not hard. The air smells wonderful, but my deep inhale doesn't help the sensation of suffocation.

Matt stands by the van, which has its rear doors open. "Can you give me a hand with this, Mira?" Matt calls to me.

"Can't," I reply turning my face away from him. "I've got to go." I reassure myself that if I was really unable to breathe I wouldn't have been able to answer him. My chest is so tight. An invisible band tightens around it.

"Mira!" Matt calls as I dash past him around to the side of the building. At the front of the building, I make a left and break into a run. It's amazing how fast I can go when I run full out. Even weaving through the people traffic on the sidewalk, I'm moving fast. Before I know it, I've covered more than twenty blocks.

It's good to run—I hadn't even realized how much I'd missed it. The deep breathing is calming me. The rain is picking up, mixing with ice. I slide and realize I'd better slow down.

Ducking into a doorway, I send Niles a message. **DON'T WORRY. JUST A LITTLE FREAKED OUT. NEED SOME SPACE TO CLEAR MY HEAD.** He'll definitely relate. **TELL THE GUYS TO LEAVE WITHOUT ME.**

It's a full-out ice storm now. The sidewalk is a sea of umbrellas, mostly black. The panic that seized me has abated.

Standing alone among this crowd of people who are completely unaware of me doesn't do anything for my sense of loneliness, though. Why am I so messed up? I'm not alone. I have Niles, Mom, Zack, Emma, the band, other friends. I know they love me—but I don't feel their love. I love them back. I know I do. But I don't *feel* it.

I'm only another ten blocks or so from Grand Central Terminal. I'll take the train home. I have enough money for a taxi from the station.

My next train home is on the lower level. I head down the wide stairs, glad to be in a warm, dry place. A loud voice announces delays on certain trains due to ice on the tracks. Mine is one of them. I pause, not sure where to go or what to do.

"Mira!" I turn toward the voice and see a young woman a little older than me. I can't recall who she is, but part of me knows she wore a ponytail the last time I saw her.

"It's me, Amy . . . from the veterans' group."

Of course! How could I forget her? She's the woman who was so friendly to me that day. I glance at her legs. Amy has no shoes on. Two curved metal pieces clink on the marble floor when she shifts position. "Hi! How are you?"

"Fine. Are you heading to the party?" she asks. She studies me more closely. "Boy, you're soaked. Will you be all right?"

A sudden chill overtakes me. My teeth chatter. Up until that moment I hadn't known how cold I really was.

"Come with me to the party," Amy says. "They'll have something warm for you to drink. First, let's get you cleaned up a little."

I leave a trail of water on the station's floor as we walk toward the bathrooms. "I ran for more than thirty blocks." I laugh lightly because it sounds so crazy. Then I go on to tell her about how blank and emotionless I've been feeling. Something about Amy— maybe it's her calm, gentle face—makes me feel I can confide in her. "Lately, I can't feel anything, and then today, when I should have felt happy, I suddenly flipped into a total panic. It doesn't make sense."

"It could be PTSD or something like it." She explains that PTSD stands for "post-traumatic stress disorder." It happens to soldiers who were in battle. My accident was certainly a huge trauma. I have some of the symptoms.

"You should probably see a therapist, and your doctor, too," she says. "You need to talk to someone. That's why I love this group so much."

Amy and I head to a small restaurant tucked away in a corner of the lower level. A mural of Italy brightens the red walls. Twenty or so people are already there. Everyone knows Amy and they're happy to see her. I notice the army officer who led the group in the hospital. All kinds of pizza are set out on a table, along with soda and punch. A DJ spins tunes, mostly radio hits.

Soon the guests start dancing. Amy rocks up and down on her two prosthetics with a guy who wears a more traditional fake leg, like the one I used to wear. Others join them on the small dance floor. All combinations of prosthetics are represented: a guy twirling in his wheelchair wears a helmet with wires attached; a young woman with a fake arm and a fake leg, like me, leans on a cane, swaying to the music; another soldier balances on two bright red legs, like the ones Amy wears. Some of the others clap in time to the music. They have one thing in common, something more than prosthetics. They are joyful—happy, laughing, full of life.

I need to have that again. More than rock stardom, more than money or fame. I want to feel joy again. I need to *feel* again. Period.

It hits me that I might never experience an emotion again. This idea hits me harder than the loss of my leg or my arm ever did. Suddenly, I don't want to be around these happy, laughing people—not if I can't share in their pleasure and fun.

As if answering my desperation, a voice comes over the station loudspeaker announcing that the tracks have been cleared and all delayed trains are once again moving. I tell Amy I have to catch my train. But she must see something in my face—I'm so anxious to leave that I'm nearly vibrating with it. We exchange phone numbers and she makes me promise to stay in touch.

Outside, in the station once more, the schedule board lists my train as leaving in twenty minutes. My track is on this lower level, just across the way, so I head for the benches to wait.

Niles sees me at the same moment I notice him sitting there. He stands, propped against his crutches. "Niles!" I cry, surprised.

"You're here!" His smile is so warm. "I was just about to give up and leave."

"What are you doing here?" I ask.

"Looking for you. I was worried. I figured you'd have to come through here eventually to get home."

"You've waited all this time?"

He glances at a paperback split open on the bench. "I have a book. I didn't mind."

We sit side by side on the bench. "Where'd you go? What happened?" he asks. I tell him that I think I had a panic attack, though it's only a guess because I've never had one before. "Why are you panicking?" Niles asks.

"I don't know who I am anymore," I say.

Niles scoffs, smiling. "Who knows who they are? Nobody— at least no one I know. Who you are keeps changing, so how can you keep track of it?"

Niles always seems so calm, sure of his identity. His words surprise me. "You don't know who you are?" I question.

"I used to be a guy who played guitar with a band. I had a crush on the band's awesome, funny, kooky lead singer, but she had a joyless boyfriend who was a real drag, so I didn't stand a chance."

"I always thought you were nice," I say.

"Yeah, but that wasn't enough," he replies. "It wasn't the same way I felt about you." We smile at each other. "Anyway . . . Then I was somebody who was in a horrific car crash and who was lucky to survive. I became a happy guy because the awesome lead singer, who was also recovering, liked me after she broke up with the idiot boyfriend. I was a guy recovering—and then I was a guy not recovering. I was a depressed guy who shut everybody out. After that, I was a guy who met the awesome lead singer again and began to feel better again. And so on."

"You've been through so many changes, too." I say.

"Yes and no," Niles says. "Through it all, I was the same on the inside. I have a center that doesn't change. I feel the same about you as I always have. Even when I shut you out, I never stopped thinking about you."

"I need to feel again, Niles. I don't know if I can go on without feeling love, even pain."

Niles takes hold of my bionic hand. His touch is so comforting. "Let's go home, Mira," he says. "My car is parked outside. I think you need some professional help to sort this out. In the meantime, I'm here."

Laying my head on his shoulder, I squeeze his hand, careful not to over-squeeze. He squeezes back, then turns his head to kiss me.

Hand in hand we head out of the station. The cold, icy rain is now mixed with snow. The wind has picked up. The snow-ice combination blows against our faces, collecting in our collars.

Niles's car is parked two blocks down. We're not dressed for this weather, but we have no choice except to put our heads down and trudge toward it. Niles's crutch slides in the slippery mix. I'm able to steady him, to keep him from toppling, which I have to do three times.

Fire trucks race somewhere. Their sirens blare. A truck backfires, spraying black soot at us, making me cough. I can't stop shivering. Finally, I see the Civic. I step between the curb and passenger-side door. Immediately, my bionic foot is in a puddle. I can feel its iciness. My left foot slides on the ice and rocks me backward onto my rear end on the sidewalk.

A blast of nausea hits my stomach. I hear Niles. "Mira!" He's reaching his hand to me.

It's the last thing I remember before being swallowed into a black hole of unconsciousness.

23

My eyes open and my mom's is the first face I see. She brushes my hair from my forehead. Her eyes are wet with tears, but she's smiling. "Mira, honey."

"I told you she'd come out of it," Dr. Hector says from somewhere behind her.

"You said her chances were good," Mom corrects him.

Dr. Hector is suddenly on the other side of me. He checks my eyes, ears, mouth, and throat with his penlight. He listens to my heart with his stethoscope. "How do you feel?" he asks.

"My head hurts—a lot," I reply. It feels like I smashed against a brick wall. My throat is also sore, but I'm not worried about that. I know from all my other surgeries that it's just from getting my fluids through the intravenous tube I'm hooked to. A monitor beeps, taking my vital signs. Oxygen is pumped up my nostrils by a contraption held in place with a wire. White gauze bandages cover my skull.

He nods and writes on his clipboard. "We'll get you something for the headache." He sighs while folding his arms. "Okay, kiddo. Here's the deal. Your mom already knows all this, but now I'm bringing you up to date. Your super-gorgeous hair, skin, and nails are a thing of the past."

"What?"

"We've changed the copper chip in your head. When your friend brought you in, you had collapsed in the street and you were just starting to come around."

I have a vague memory of a nurse washing my face with a cloth. I half recall people rushing around, sticking me with needles, rushing up and down hallways while I'm strapped to a gurney. In my mind it's dreamlike, but apparently it happened.

"This new chip is much less powerful. Your blood isn't circulating as fast. You won't be producing so much more of it. The old chip was too much for your bodily systems to handle. It was putting you on overload."

"Will I be able to feel emotions again?" I ask.

Dr. Hector furrows his brow, confused. I explain the emotional blankness I've been experiencing. He nods, taking notes. "This is interesting," he says. "It's possible that blood flow was directed away from your limbic system to empower other neural pathways. We know that the limbic system affects emotion, although we can't exactly pinpoint where in the brain all emotion stems from. Injuries to the frontal lobes of the brain can cause a flattening of affect in patients."

"Flattening of affect?" I ask.

"A dullness, a lack of emotionality," Dr. Hector explains.

"Yes! That's it! Will that go away?"

"I don't know," Dr. Hector says. "We'll watch it carefully, though. Your friend told me you thought you had had a panic attack?"

"It felt like it might be," I say. "Another friend thought it could be post-traumatic stress."

"We'll be watching for that, too." He writes a script which he hands to Mom. "That's the name, number, and email of a psychiatrist associated with these medical trials. Set up an appointment for Mira."

This time I don't object. When you need help, you need help. People might not change, but they learn.

"And what about the panic attacks or PTSD?" Mom asks.

"It's related to her brain function and it could be caused by her situation as well," Dr. Hector says. "Both things are about to change, so we'll keep an eye on it. There are going to be a lot of changes coming."

• • •

Niles's old dented Civic pulls into the parking area near the lake. Through the falling snow he walks across the road, bent a little over his cane, his backpack slung over his shoulder. Zack is beside him, his head thrown back to catch the flakes on his tongue. "Let Project Snowman begin," Niles says when they reach me.

I come in for a kiss with my somewhat chapped lips. My hair has flopped a bit and now my nails crack sometimes. And in the cold, my lips chap. The reduced copper chip inside me still works, but I'm not operating at "ultimate capacity."

"You two stop that. It's gross," Zack says.

Although Zack and I do most of the snow rolling, Niles collects pine branches for arms, rocks for eyes, and he's brought a carrot for a nose. Before too long we have a lumpy, fat snowman. "He's not perfect, but he's ours," Niles says. He takes a picture of Zack and me with our snowman, and checks the time. "We have to leave for practice in fifteen minutes," he says. The band is playing smaller venues again, and my swallowed-an-amplifier voice has simmered down. I've also had to go back to learn guitar, since my ability to memorize through visualization is mostly gone. Niles is teaching me, which is fun. He's finally come back to the band, though our dancing days are over—he sits on a stool to play.

Zack sees a friend from school coming down the road pulling a sled and runs off to talk to him.

Niles asks me to get his backpack from the ground, since it's difficult for him to bend. "I have a present for you."

"I love presents!"

"Yeah, well, I hope you like this. I made it myself." My present is wrapped in blue tissue paper.

Niles has taken a photo of the two of us dancing—he's swinging me into a twirl and our hands are interlocked—and made another statue, scaled down to about eight inches each, of the two of us.

"I love it!" I say honestly.

"It's how we used to look," he says. "I'm going to miss that printer when I graduate."

"While you still have the printer, could you make another figure?" I request.

"Sure. What picture should I use?"

"This one," I say, tilting my phone to show him. It's a shot of Niles and me that Emma took during a break at our last practice. We're seated side by side. Niles's crutches rest against his knee. In the picture Niles is showing me how to play the bridge in our latest song. We're intent on what we're doing, not smiling for the camera.

"Why do you like this picture?" Niles asks. "We're just sitting there, and we're never that serious."

"Because it shows us as we are," I say. "See how we lean toward each other?"

He nods, looking at me with a smile in his eyes.

Niles takes my bionic hand and pulls me closer for a kiss. I feel such a wash of love—for Niles, for my mom and Zack, for Emma and the band and the snow and the lake—that, for a moment, I'm overwhelmed. So much has changed, and so much is changing, but right now, I know it's going to be okay. With every particle of myself, bionic and organic, I *feel* it.

ACKNOWLEDGMENTS

Thanks to my always astute, supportive, and hardworking editor, Erin Black, for all her guidance.

ABOUT THE AUTHOR

Suzanne Weyn is the acclaimed author of *Faces of the Dead*, *Dr. Frankenstein's Daughters*, *Distant Waves*, and *Reincarnation*, as well as *The Bar Code Tattoo*, *The Bar Code Rebellion*, and *The Bar Code Prophecy*. She is also the author of the Haunted Museum series for younger readers. Suzanne lives in upper New York State, and you can visit her online at www.suzanneweynbooks.com.